"You've had me under *surveillance?*"

Rachel continued, "Anyone would think you're vetting me as a potential mistress." She'd been so busy keeping tabs on *Matthew* that it had never occurred to her to look over her shoulder!

"Lover." The soft word caressed her senses like a fur glove. "You could only be my mistress if I was already married. Since I'm not, that would make you my prospective lover rather than my kept woman."

As Rachel scrabbled for a sufficiently devastating answer, Matthew added, "But why set your sights so low? I could be checking out your suitability as a potential wife...."

Susan Napier

THE MISTRESS DECEPTION

Passion™

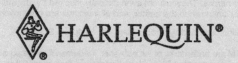

HARLEQUIN®

TORONTO • NEW YORK • LONDON
AMSTERDAM • PARIS • SYDNEY • HAMBURG
STOCKHOLM • ATHENS • TOKYO • MILAN • MADRID
PRAGUE • WARSAW • BUDAPEST • AUCKLAND

ISBN 0-373-12111-3

THE MISTRESS DECEPTION

First North American Publication 2000.

Copyright © 1999 by Susan Napier.

This edition published by arrangement with Harlequin Books S.A.

® and TM are trademarks of the publisher. Trademarks indicated with ® are registered in the United States Patent and Trademark Office, the Canadian Trade Marks Office and in other countries.

Visit us at www.eHarlequin.com

Printed in U.S.A.

CHAPTER ONE

'EXCUSE me—Mr Riordan...?'

Matthew Riordan's dark head jerked up at the interruption and he directed an impatient frown at the middle-aged woman hovering in the doorway of his borrowed office.

'I'm sorry to disturb you...' she said, undeterred by the scowl on his narrow, long-boned face. She advanced towards his desk, a large manila envelope held out between her fingertips. 'I know you asked me to deal with your father's personal correspondence until he's well enough to do it himself, but—well...I think this is probably something that you would prefer to handle yourself...'

Matt's abstraction was banished as he rocked back in his leather chair, his thick eyebrows rising at the sight of his father's unflappable secretary looking so ill at ease.

Was that a *blush* on those leathery cheeks? he wondered incredulously, his dark brown eyes sharpening behind the lenses of his round gold and tortoiseshell spectacles.

For over three decades—since before Matt was born—she had serenely guarded his father's Auckland office, more than a match for Kevin Riordan's rough-and-tumble personality and the raffish nature of many of his employees and customers in the early years of his company. The former rubbish-man turned scrap-dealer and recycling mogul, now owner of New Zealand's largest waste-disposal conglomerate, had rewarded her mental toughness and unflagging loyalty with his boisterous respect, smugly boasting to all and sundry that nothing could fluster his redoubtable Mary.

His confidence had proved justified two days earlier, when Mary had investigated a thud from his office and discovered her employer in the throes of a heart attack. Instantly conquering her shock, she had phoned for an ambulance and proceeded to calmly administer CPR until the medical team arrived. Then she had busied herself telephoning his wife and son, faxing his second-in-command, who was in Tokyo on business, and discreetly fending off speculation and rumours as she postponed appointments and rearranged meetings.

Now, she gingerly placed the neatly slit foolscap envelope on the desk in front of Matt and scuttled backwards.

'What is it—a letter-bomb?' he commented drily, and Mary regained enough of her steely poise to give him a stern look, admonishing him for his flippancy.

Matt laid down his pen and pulled off his glasses, tossing them onto the blotter. His eyes felt gritty with fatigue as he picked up the envelope, noting the plainly typed address with the words 'Strictly Personal' thickly underlined several times. He tipped it up by one corner and three glossy photographs slid face-down across the desk.

He flipped one over and his eyebrows scooted up in puzzled surprise.

The glossy black and white photograph had been taken at a party two weeks ago—a profile shot of Matt leaning over the hand of a tall, voluptuous woman whose long, strapless glittering white gown looked as if it had been applied to her pneumatic curves with a spray gun.

He and the woman were both holding champagne glasses and smiling brilliantly, but the flattering picture didn't tell the full story.

The photograph didn't show the long, painted nails digging painfully into his skin, punishing him for the parody of a kiss he had just planted on the back of her hand. Nor did it reveal that Matt had been dangerously drunk, sullen and obstreperous.

He hadn't been aware that there was anyone taking photographs that night, although in the circumstances that was hardly surprising, but he doubted that Merrilyn Freeman, their over-anxious hostess, would have jeopardised the exclusivity of her private dinner party by inviting a professional photographer along. The harsh contrasts and grainy texture suggested the print had been blown up from a much smaller negative.

It was also perfectly innocuous—nothing to give Mary Marcus reason to treat the envelope as if it was an unexploded bomb.

In the course of his business and social life Matt had been photographed in similar poses with numerous women of his acquaintance. He could see no reason why anyone would want to mail this one to his father, except, perhaps, as an attempt to curry favour...

Matt flipped over the other photographs and his complacent assumption exploded in his face. He stiffened, the breath hissing between his clenched teeth.

To his intense chagrin he could feel the warmth flooding into his face. Although he didn't look up he was excruciatingly aware of Mary's disapproving gaze as she made good her escape, closing the door behind her with a definitive snap that sealed him in with the smoking ruins of his reputation as a gentleman.

Thank God he could rely on her to keep her mouth shut!

His mouth compressed into a thin line, Matt studied the evidence of his betrayal.

In the first photograph Matt was sitting bare-chested on the edge of a rumpled bed, facing towards the camera, his smooth torso sculpted by the soft light from a bedside lamp. The woman in the strapless dress was kneeling on the floor between his splayed legs, the white sequins of her gown a glittering contrast to the black fabric of Matt's formal trousers where his knees pressed against her flanks, trapping her in the quintessential pose of female sexual submission. He was looking down at her bent head, his palms cupping her skull, fingers threaded into her feathery, short-cropped hair, while hers were out of sight of the camera's intrusive eye…from the position of her bent elbows, obviously busy in his lap!

God!

Matt's flush deepened, his blood pressure spiking as he transferred his stunned gaze to the second picture. Here the roles of submission and domination were dramatically reversed. This time Matt was lying flat on his back on the bed, the muscles of his deep chest straining against the pull of his arms stretched over his head, his crossed wrists bound to the head of the brass bedstead with the narrow silk cummerbund he had been wearing in the earlier photo. Straddling his lower belly was the Valkyrie, flaunting a vast expanse of smooth, creamy skin unmarked by tan-lines, her knees digging into his lower ribcage, her spectacular breasts hovering invitingly above his pillowed head as she arched up to secure his bonds. The crowning salacious touch was the thin black leather whip which lay coiled on the bed beside them.

Matt cursed, his alcohol-hazed memories warring with the erotic images before him. His expression tightened as he shifted uncomfortably in his chair, trying to ease the treacherous tautening in another part of his anatomy.

He was furious, and aroused—and furious at himself for being aroused. He had been manipulated—his pride scraped raw, his privacy violated—and instead of being disgusted he was getting turned on!

He raked his fingers inside the empty envelope, grimly

unsurprised to find that there was no accompanying message.

No message was needed. Matt knew exactly what form the blackmail would take.

The bitch had set him up!

And to think that he had sent her flowers afterwards, to thank her for preventing him from making a complete drunken ass of himself at the party...an expensive sheaf of yellow roses and a polite, handwritten note which had skilfully disguised his chagrin that *she* should be his rescuer and, later in that guest-house bedroom, sole witness to his humiliating weakness.

Except it was now painfully obvious that she had *not* been the sole witness!

Matt pinched the narrow bridge of his nose, castigating himself for his gullibility. How could he have allowed himself to trust her? He had been suspicious of her from the first day they had ever met, and even tanked to the eyeballs he had recognised the cool antipathy she had exuded when Merrilyn had anxiously thrust them into each other's company. It had been partly the desire to smash through that frigid aloofness which had goaded him into baiting her the way that he had.

And now she thought she had it within her grasp to extract the perfect revenge.

Well, he might have been an easy target drunk, but—sober—he was going to show her how very difficult he could be!

He glanced at the smudged date-stamp on the manila envelope, his eyebrows snapping together when he realised what it meant. He leaned forward and punched in Mary's extension number on his telephone.

'Mr Riordan's office—'

'Mary, when did this envelope arrive in the office?' he

demanded, his abrupt urgency overriding any potential embarrassment.

'The day before yesterday—in the morning,' Mary replied, after a small hesitation to think out the sequence of events. 'I always slit open Mr Riordan's personal mail for him as soon as it arrives, and put the stack on his desk...but of course I never look at the contents unless he expressly asks me to—'

'So this has just been lying around—open—on Dad's desk for the past two days?' interrupted Matt, sweating bullets.

'Well, yes...but with Mr Stiller not due back from Tokyo until later in the week, only the cleaners and I have had access to Mr Riordan's office,' Mary pointed out.

Matt's tension eased a notch at the reminder of his cousin's absence. Both only children, he and Neville Stiller had spent a lot of time in each other's company while growing up, but as adults their relationship was far from cordial.

Neville, who had worked at KR Industries ever since he'd left high school, had been appointed Chief Executive five years ago, and was generally expected to take over as General Manager when his uncle retired. Matt, on the other hand, had been actively discouraged from following directly in his father's footsteps. Instead he had been educated, guided and groomed for the job which now consumed most of his waking hours—chairman of the family's holding company, which controlled multimillion-dollar investments in both the local and international share markets.

Matt had long accepted that there was no place for him in the flourishing business which had been the cornerstone of his father's fortune, but Neville remained intensely protective of the power-base he had carved out for himself, quick to resent any advice or expression of interest in the firm as an attempt to undermine his position as Kevin Riordan's successor.

If this pivotal deal had not demanded Neville's continuing presence in Tokyo, Matt didn't doubt that he would have rushed back to commandeer the General Manager's office.

Firmly ensconced in the seat of power, Neville would have had few qualms about nosing through his stricken uncle's private correspondence, and if he *had* come across the photos how he would have gloated over the knowledge that his cousin had been caught, quite literally, with his pants down!

Matt cringed at the thought. As it was, Neville had had little choice but to grudgingly accept Matt's offer to hold the fort until he had concluded his complex negotiations with a Japanese industrial waste management company with whom KR Industries was planning a joint venture.

Suddenly Matt was hit by another, even more devastating worry.

'Do you know if Dad had time to look at his private mail before he had his heart attack?' he grated.

Mary's sharply indrawn breath recognised the ugly implication. 'I suppose he may have done,' she admitted slowly. 'We went through the business mail together first, as usual, and he dictated a few urgent letters, but…yes—it's possible that he started going through his own mail while I was typing up the letters. But since that envelope was the largest, I would have put it at the bottom of his pile…'

They both knew that that was little consolation. The brash personality shaped by Kevin Riordan's poverty-stricken childhood viewed size as an important indicator of status. 'Restraint' was not a word which figured large in his vocabulary. If he had decided to read his mail he was likely to have reasoned that the bigger the envelope the more interesting the contents.

In this case he would have been right!

Matt's dark eyes narrowed to glittering black slits, a faint tic pulsing on the hard temple above his left eyebrow. His left hand clenched on the receiver, the spare flesh whitening over his knuckles and around the broad gold band on his ring finger.

'Mary—bring me a plain foolscap envelope!' he ordered, and slammed down the phone.

He dragged a blank writing tablet towards him and picked up his fountain pen to scrawl a slashing message in his trademark green ink across the page.

When Mary appeared with his request he transferred the photographs and the folded message into the new envelope and addressed it in aggressive block letters.

'See that it goes out immediately,' he said, pushing the sealed envelope across the desk.

'By courier, or post?'

His smile was unpleasant.

'Courier.' He wanted the blackmailer's mental suffering to start as soon as possible.

Mary looked at the address, her poker-face breaking up as she raised concerned grey eyes to his. 'Don't you think you should—'

'Just do it!'

Her mouth snapped shut at his unprecedented rudeness. Her chin lifted and she turned on her heel, her rigid, bony back a silent reproach. Matt was irresistibly reminded that her staunch loyalty to his father had always also extended to himself.

'I'm sorry, Mary,' he apologised swiftly, his deep voice resonant with sincerity as he ran his fingers through his thick wavy hair, disciplined into a conservative cut that flattered the long bones of his face. 'I didn't mean to shout. I'm not angry at *you*. What with keeping my mother company at the hospital and trying to juggle things here, as well as my own job, I haven't had much sleep over the past two nights and I'm afraid my temper's suffered accordingly. But as you said before—this is something that I need to handle myself...'

As a boy he had always been quick to admit fault and offer amends, thought Mary, and as a man he was equally ruthless with his failings. In fact sometimes she felt he took too *much* responsibility upon himself...

'I just hope you know what you're doing,' she murmured.

'Oh, I know exactly what I'm doing,' he told her with a savage smile. 'I'm turning the tables on an extortionist.

'I have a feeling that I may turn out to have a gift for blackmail!'

CHAPTER TWO

RACHEL BLAIR sat at the kitchen table sipping her morning coffee and glowering at the letter in her hand.

'Hello, what are you doing up so early?' Her elder sister came bustling through the door, dressed in her nurse's uniform and carrying an armful of crumpled sheets and damp towels. 'I thought you were going to leave it one more day before you went back to work.' She vanished into the adjacent laundry and Rachel could hear her lifting and closing the lid of the temperamental washing machine and cranking the dial around.

'I felt perfectly fine when I woke up so I changed my mind,' Rachel called to her through the archway. The mild headache niggling at her consciousness she preferred to attribute to the letter in her hand rather than the lingering after-effects of her ailment.

'Hmm.' Robyn reappeared in the doorway and gave her a professional once-over. 'Just make sure you don't overdo it. Your immune system's probably still not back to full strength.'

'It was only a virus,' Rachel pointed out. 'I've finished my course of antibiotics and my cold is pretty much gone— see?' She sniffed to show that the clogged airways of the past few days had cleared.

Robyn shook her blonde head in bafflement. 'I don't know how you managed to catch the flu in the middle of Auckland's hottest summer on record. No one else we know has it...'

With an effort Rachel managed not to blush.

'I guess I'm just ahead of my time,' she said airily. 'The doctor said I have the type they'll be offering a vaccine for this winter.'

Fortunately Robyn was easily diverted from her speculation on the source of the infection.

'Maybe if you're lucky they'll name it after you,' she grinned.

Rachel could think of someone far more deserving of the honour of being commemorated as an irksome germ!

'Type-Rachel flu? Do you think I could ask for royalties?' She grinned back, and the resemblance between the sisters was suddenly pronounced, even though, superficially, they looked as different as chalk and cheese.

At forty, Robyn was still as slim and petite as she had been as a teenager, her ash-blonde hair and big blue eyes lending her a doll-like air of feminine fragility which was belied by her job as a hard-working practice nurse.

Ten years her junior, Rachel towered over her sister, and most other women of her acquaintance. Her wide shoulders and full bust would have made her top-heavy if it hadn't been for the broadly rounded hips flaring below her neat waist, and her long, firmly muscled legs. Her triangular face, framed by a spiky, razor-cut cap of hair the colour of burnt toffee, thickly lashed hazel eyes and thin, determined mouth possessed strength of character rather than beauty... but unfortunately people often tended to judge her from the neck down!

She knew that her curvy, hour-glass shape rendered her almost a cartoon-figure of female pulchritude, the living embodiment of countless male fantasies.

It had been rough coping with the unwonted sexual attention when she was young, but she had determined very early on not to let her overtly sexy body image dictate the path of her life. She had fought hard to be her own person, and with maturity had perfected subtle strategies to control the perceptions and prejudices of those around her—dressing casually, in loose, multi-layered clothing, and cultivating a robust good humour which was the opposite of seductive. Fortunately her height and superior strength gave her a physical edge whenever her defensive strategies proved too subtle for over-active male libidos.

'I doubt it—though you'd probably have hordes of guys clamouring to be personally infected,' chuckled Robyn. Thanks to the considerable age gap between them, and the fact that she had been happily married to Simon Fox for over twenty years, she had never been jealous of her sister's effect on men.

A rattling mechanical hiccup sounded behind her and she darted through to give the washing machine a well-practised kick of encouragement.

Rachel rolled her eyes and returned her brooding attention to her unwelcome letter.

She was getting fed up with this petty campaign of harassment. At first she had dismissed the escalating stream of annoyances as an unfortunate run of back luck, but too many coincidences had piled up, and now her suspicions condensed into certainty.

It was typical of her unknown harasser to hide behind a faceless bureaucracy. Whoever had it in for her was a coward—but very a clever one, initiating trouble but never following it through to a point where Rachel might have a chance to identify the source.

A low growl of frustration purred in the back of her throat.

'What's the matter?' asked Robyn, drifting back to the accompaniment of noisily hissing water pipes.

'The council has received a tip that I'm running a business from this address,' Rachel paraphrased in disgust.

'They're warning me that they're going to investigate and I could be prosecuted for carrying on a non-complying activity.'

'It must be some mistake,' said Robyn, tucking a shoulder-length strand of hair back into the smooth French twist she wore at work.

'You think so? And was it also a mistake when the phone company was told the same thing and tried to charge me a higher line rental? And when the tax department decided to audit me because someone phoned their hotline and told them I had an undeclared second income? Or when I didn't get any mail for two weeks and suddenly discovered that the post office had been advised to redirect my mail to a house which just happened to be the residence of a motor-cycle gang?'

Robyn put a hand to her mouth. 'Oh! That reminds me—Bethany said something arrived for you yesterday afternoon by courier. You were having a bath and she was just leaving for basketball practice so she just signed for it and took off with it in her bag. She forgot all about it until this morning.'

She crossed the small, sunny kitchen and fetched the bubble-wrapped plastic courier bag which had been tucked with some other papers behind the telephone on the bench, handing it to her sister.

She glanced at the watch pinned to her breast and let out a little huff. 'I hope Bethany's out of that bathroom—I'm sure when you offered to put us up for a few weeks you didn't expect to have to put up with a teenager who showers twice a day for twenty minutes at a time! I do wish you'd let us pay something towards the water and power, as well as the groceries.'

Rachel paused in the act of ripping into the zip-locked seam of the bag. 'Don't be silly. Just be thankful that

Bethany's into cleanliness, not some ghastly grunge kick. It's not as if I have to pay rent, or a mortgage. I've loved having you to stay.' There was a hint of wistfulness in her hazel eyes. Since David had died two years ago there had been no one special in her life, no one who was critical to her happiness—or she to theirs. Usually she kept herself looking resolutely to the future, but these last few days of enforced rest had given her time to dwell on all the 'might have beens.'

She shook off the cruelly unproductive thoughts. 'I just wish that Simon wasn't coming back so soon and whisking you both so far away,' she said lightly.

'We're only moving to Bangkok—not the moon,' Robyn chided her bracingly. Simon, who worked for a multinational chemical company, was being transferred to Thailand to help build a new manufacturing plant. While he had flown out there to meet his new boss, choose their company-paid accommodation and register Bethany to attend the local International School, his wife and daughter had been packing up and selling their Auckland home and arranging to ship their belongings.

'We get an annual home-leave, and, anyway, I hope you'll come up and have a holiday with us. You did say that Westons had some huge contract in the offing that might let you give up your day job!'

Rachel gave a rueful laugh. Her work as a massage therapist and fitness trainer was actually carried out in the early morning or late afternoon and evening, so that she could devote the business hours to the security company which she had inherited from David. No one had been more astonished than herself when she had discovered that her fiancé of six months had altered his will to leave her not only his townhouse but also his fifty-one percent share of the se-

curity company which he and his brother Frank, a fellow
ex-policeman, had bought.

Although Weston Security Services had possessed a
loyal core of clients at the time of David's death, it had
also been carrying a heavy debt-load, and at first, woefully
aware of her ignorance, Rachel had been content to remain
a silent partner. But as the business had continued to struggle she had realised that it would be a betrayal of David's
trust to watch his cherished dream die without lifting a
finger to help.

It hadn't been an investment that he had given her in his
will so much as a part of himself. *She* might doubt herself,
but David had always had faith in her ability to tackle new
challenges. To that end she had used her stake in the company to persuade Frank to give her an active role in managing the business. She had waived a salary, preferring to
see the money invested in new staff and equipment, and
lived off her freelance earnings from two city gyms and a
physiotherapy practice.

It had been a steep learning curve, and although Rachel
had made plenty of mistakes, her hands-on method of training wasn't proving the disaster that Frank had feared it
would be. In the last few months the company turn-over
had shown a promising improvement, but a balloon repay-
ment was looming on the loan, and meeting the debt was
largely reliant on a major corporate contract which Frank
seemed to be confident was already in the bag. Rachel was
not so sanguine.

'I think it'll be a while before I can afford to do that,'
she sighed. 'Frank says that trust and respect build slowly
in the security business, and being a woman in a male-
dominated industry makes it that much more difficult to get
accepted—'

She was interrupted as her sister took another surreptitious look at her watch and dashed for the door with a squawk of dismay.

Rachel returned to ripping open the zip-lock bag. Her birthday wasn't far away, and she wondered with a lift of her spirits whether someone had sent her an early present.

Her eager anticipation drained abruptly away as she withdrew some photographs paper-clipped to the back of a scrawled note in green ink which slanted across the page, arrogantly ignoring the ruled lines. She washed down her disappointment with her rapidly cooling coffee as she scanned the jolting words.

Did you really think I would let you use me as your free ride to riches?

Of the two of us you're obviously the more photogenic—a fact which I'm sure the tabloid press will be quick to exploit if these, or any even more explicit, are put into circulation. I always knew you were centrefold material, but while the resultant notoriety might well annoy me, it won't destroy me. Unlike you. What will happen to Westons' reputation for probity and discretion when your corporate clients find out that their security rests in the whip-hand of a blowsy, over-blown dominatrix who looks as if she'd be more at home in a brothel than a boardroom?

Sorry, doll.

You lose.

A mouthful of lukewarm coffee was stranded in her mouth as her throat clogged with shock. Her cup crashed down into its saucer as she unclipped the photographs and fanned them out in her hands like oversized cards.

'Oh, God!' She choked, spewing coffee droplets across

the table in her spluttering horror, dropping the photographs as if they were hot coals.

'Oh, *God*!' Rachel's horror deepened to bone-bruising humiliation, the outrageous insults in the note suddenly making sickening sense. There was no signature, but she didn't need one. She knew instantly who to blame for the outrage.

She shuddered, pressing her shaking hands to hot cheeks as she looked down at the shameful photographs. Yes, she had knelt between his legs to unfasten his trousers...but this picture gave the impression that she had been—that she had done it in order to *pleasure* him. The heavy-lidded smile on his face certainly seemed to suggest that she'd been succeeding, whereas in reality she had been cursing a blue streak that his formal trousers had buttons rather than a zip—which she would have cheerfully used to castrate him! If he had gained any pleasure from what she had been doing, then it was purely his own warped mind that had created it.

And the other one—*God!*...that didn't look anything *like* the way it had actually happened, either. Why—these pictures made her look as if she had been a willing participant in some kind of disgusting sexual perversion, rather than the good Samaritan which she had been dragooned into playing.

But good Samaritans didn't roll around naked on a bed with those they rescued, the devil whispered in her ear.

Rachel shook her head, still dazed by the shock of seeing herself portrayed in the role of sexual predator. It was so fundamentally at odds with her character that it would almost be funny if it wasn't so humiliating. The photographs were slanderously misleading. The circumstantial evidence might trumpet otherwise, but the situation had actually been completely innocent.

Well, perhaps not *completely*, she forced herself to admit as her mind replayed the images of that night. It had definitely not been her finest hour, but Matthew Riordan was to blame for everything that had happened. The whole unsavoury incident had been entirely his own fault!

So how dared he? How *dared* he now turn around and threaten to slander *her* with the evidence of *his* indiscretion! She had never said a word to anyone—not even Frank or Merrilyn—about what had happened that night after they had left the party. In spite of the pressure to gossip she had uttered not a single, solitary syllable. For *his* sake!

And this was how he repaid her for her kindness! One feeble bunch of flowers and this...this *outrage*!

The blood boiled in her veins as she looked at the note and one word suddenly jumped out at her. Blowsy. *Blowsy?*

Her hazel eyes turned a ferocious green. She could shrug off his groundless accusation that she belonged in a brothel as sheer malice, but how dared he call her blowsy? He hadn't had any objections to her *over-blown* 'centrefold' of a body when he'd been begging her to make love to him, had he?

She was infuriated to feel her breasts tighten at the memory of his words, of the uninhibited way that he had expressed his desire as they had wrestled on the bed. As drunk as he'd been she had thought that he would be incapable of physical arousal, and hadn't he taken great delight in proving her wrong! But then, maybe he hadn't been quite so drunk as he had made out. Maybe it had all been a big act in order to lure her into just such a compromising position while some sleazy photographer snapped away from the closet.

Her eyes went unwillingly back to the most explicit photograph and hot chills fizzled in her belly. It was her body which was flaunted centre-stage, but no one could deny that

Matthew Riordan made a pretty impressive supporting act. He wasn't quite as tall as Rachel, but with his clothes off he had been larger than she had expected, in *all* ways... His lean body had a ripped quality, all muscle with little softening body fat, and the raw strength in the muscle-dense arms and thighs had taken her by surprise. At Westons she was used to seeing security guards shaped like weightlifters, but Matthew Riordan's smooth, sleek body had an understated elegance that merely hinted at the power that lay sheathed beneath his skin.

The dirty rat! What a hypocrite he was—the cool, cultivated, highly respectable Matthew Riordan, scion of his wealthy family and controller of a substantial chunk of the New Zealand economy...

Well, the arrogant pig needn't think he could control *her*. She mentally tossed her head. Let everyone find out that the real Matthew Riordan was a sleazy manipulator, without a scrap of moral conscience or a shred of human decency.

She looked at the photo of them lying on the bed and groaned, covering her hot face with her hands. In the end, would it matter which one of them was exposed as the liar? Any mud she threw was going to stick to both of them, and, while he had unlimited resources with which to whitewash himself clean, she had virtually none.

He had already proved as cunning as a snake and as lucky as the devil, she thought, peeking through her fingers again. He couldn't have arranged that pose better if he had employed a Hollywood director to choreograph the sexy scene. The way they were posed made the most of her abundant breasts, her jutting nipples almost brushing his parted lips as she stretched above him to tighten his bindings. He needed only to lift his head slightly and...

Oh, no! She clamped down on the unruly urge to wander

down *that* tortuous memory lane. She wasn't going to be made to feel more of a sexual deviant than she did already. She struggled to fix her mind on more important matters. The most threatening implication in the note as far as she was concerned was that there were even *more* explicit photographs in existence.

Her eyes fell on the whip and she gave a little hiccup of hysteria. Admittedly she hadn't been exactly alert to her wider surroundings while their tussle had been going on, but how could she have missed noticing *that*? The whole tenor of the scene implied that she was about to use it once she had rendered her victim helpless. As if she would ever use a whip against another human being! she thought hotly.

Although, come to think of it, at the moment the idea did have a certain sadistic appeal. Her pale pink lips pulled unconsciously back from her white teeth as she savoured the vengeful notion. Oh, yes, she mused—if Matthew Riordan and a handy whip should present themselves to her right now she might well take a great deal of pleasure in lashing the gloating smirk off his face.

So he thought he had won this dirty little game of one-upmanship, did he…?

'Hi, Rachel, whatcha looking at?'

Rachel gave a frightened little yelp as Bethany bounced into the kitchen, her freckled face scrubbed squeaky clean, her budding breasts thrusting against her dark green school tunic as she leaned over the table.

'Mum said you were opening the courier's package. What was in it? Photos? Can I see?'

As Rachel frantically tried to push the prints back into the bag Bethany hooked one away. Fortunately for Rachel's madly thundering heart it was the innocuous shot from the party.

'Hey. Wow!' Bethany's green-gold eyes rounded in admiration. 'What a babe! Who is he?'

'No one.' Rachel tried to grab the photograph back, but Bethany danced out of reach with a chuckle.

'You look pretty hot, too. Nothing like your usual maiden-aunt get-ups. You look as if you're about to explode out of that dress! Were you trying to vamp him? He looks pretty vamped to me.'

'Bethany—' Rachel's protest held a breathless note of desperation that only egged her tormentor on.

'So, who is he?' Bethany teased, her face splitting on a grin, her long blonde ponytail dancing across her slender shoulders as she tilted her head. 'A new boyfriend?'

Rachel fired up. 'Definitely *not*!'

Bethany evidently thought her violent rejection a bit overdone. 'He looks a bit younger than you,' she said slyly. 'Is he your secret toyboy…?'

Rachel bristled with all the dignity of her thirty years. 'Hardly. I *believe* he's about twenty-six!' she snapped. Certainly old enough to have learned more respect for women. Perhaps she would be the one to teach him some manners!

'Mmm. A pity he wears glasses, but I guess you can't have everything, huh? At least his bod is nice, and he has that eat-you-up smile. And I don't suppose he wears his glasses in bed…or haven't you got him that far yet?'

Rachel went hot all over.

'Beth-a-ny!'

Thank God those other photos were safely out of sight!

'Oops, I forgot—personality is more important than looks, right?' The girl giggled. 'At least, that's what you and Mum are always telling me. So—how sexy is his personality?'

'Somewhat less than a slug's,' Rachel blurted out through her gritted teeth.

Bethany laughed in disbelief. 'Oh, yeah? Then why are

you looking at him as if you'd like to take a bite out of him?'

'Appearances can be deceptive,' she warned. 'For instance, you look like an innocent fifteen-year-old schoolgirl, when we both know you're actually the devil incarnate.'

Bethany raised and lowered her eyebrows. 'Sounds kinky. Does that have anything to do with being carnal?'

Rachel bit back a reluctant smile. 'You know it doesn't, you evil child.'

Not only was Bethany highly intelligent, but thanks to her frank upbringing she also had a lively understanding of the world around her. Although Rachel sometimes found her sophistication unnerving, in her heart she thanked God that Bethany wasn't as naive and wretchedly vulnerable as Rachel had been at her age.

'So, are you going to tell me all about your pin-up boy?' asked Bethany, finally handing the photograph back and clattering from cupboard to fridge to fix herself a large bowl of cereal and milk.

'He's no pin-up, believe me,' Rachel said darkly, ramming the resealed bubble-pack deep into her capacious shoulder-bag, hoping the contents would be creased into oblivion. 'He's a slimy, spiteful, scum-sucking, foul-minded, flatulent, male chauvinistic swine with a brain the size of a quark and an ego the size of Mount Everest.'

Bethany's mouth fell open and Rachel flushed as she realised that she had let herself get carried away by her inner rage. But how good it had felt to snarl it out loud! She hastily summoned a weak grin to show that she had only been joking.

'Of course—that's on his *good* days.'

'Uh, sure…' In spite of her evident curiosity Bethany wisely decided not to tease for an answer as to what the mystery man was like on his *bad* days. She crunched on her cereal, sending sidelong looks at Rachel as she got up and absently washed out her coffee cup, her mind still shell-shocked by Matthew Riordan's underhanded attack.

'Um, Rachel…I—we get on really well together, you and I…don't we?'

'Mmm?' She couldn't just ignore his vicious threat and expect it to go away. He had the potential to make her life a misery. 'Oh—yes, of course we do,' she said warmly.

'And you know how you always say how much you like having me around—you know, when Mum and Dad go away on holiday and I come and stay here with you…?'

Rachel shook out a teatowel. She knew what it was like to be a helpless victim and she had no intention of ever letting it happen again. 'What?' She struggled to make sense of what Bethany was saying. 'Oh, yes, I do—you're great company.'

'Well…how would you feel if I was—you know—around a lot more. Like…maybe…all the time…'

Rachel's attention snapped fully back to the young girl at the table.

'All the time?' Her voice sharpened as she realised what her niece was asking. 'You mean, you living here…with me? Permanently?' Her heart expanded tightly in her chest so that she could hardly breathe as Bethany nodded. 'But, Beth,' she protested weakly, 'you're going to be living in Bangkok—'

Bethany abandoned the table, eager to argue her case.

'Just because Dad has to work there doesn't mean I have to be dragged away from all my friends—I mean, what if I don't like the school?' she said in a rush. 'I won't know anyone, I don't know the language—'

'Beth, it's an English-speaking school,' Rachel pointed out gently. 'There'll be teenagers like you there from all around the world. They're all in the same boat, and you'll soon make new friends—'

'But I like my old ones! I love the school I go to now…and what about my yachting? I bet I won't be able to bike down to the harbour and go sailing on my own in Thailand!'

'Oh, Beth, if you feel like this you should talk to your parents—'

'I have,' she gulped. 'But they don't listen. They keep telling me I'll adjust. But what if I *can't*? What if I really, really, *really* hate it over there? Mum and Dad wouldn't let me come back on my own, but if I was coming to live with you, then they couldn't say no, could they?' She bit her lip and her voice wavered. 'Unless you don't want me to…you think I'd be in the way…'

A lump rose in Rachel's throat and she had to swallow hard to stop herself bursting into tears. She longed to let her emotions rule, to sweep Bethany fiercely to her breast and assure her that of *course* she wouldn't be in the way, that she would *always* be welcome into Rachel's home and heart.

But she knew she couldn't. There were bigger issues at stake. She took a deep breath.

'Oh, darling, I know how you're feeling.' She cupped Bethany's long face with her strong fingers and smiled brightly into her woeful eyes, hoping to phrase her rejection in a way that wouldn't irreparably damage their very precious relationship. 'I know you're scared about stepping out into the unknown, but you're not alone. Don't you think that your parents are finding this move a bit scary, too?'

Bethany blinked at the sudden shift in her perspective. 'Mum and Dad?'

'Of course—they're leaving behind all their friends, too. It's going to be especially tough for your dad—he has to step into a new job in a new country with colleagues he doesn't know, while displaying the confidence and authority that people expect of his new position. And your mum—she has to give up a job she really loves and revert to being a full-time housewife in a community where she doesn't know a soul. But together you'll get through it. The three of you are a *team*...'

Bethany was quick to pick up the underlying message. 'So you won't let me come and live with you, even if I'm horribly homesick?' she said in a thin, high voice.

Rachel braced herself against the mixture of hurt and resentment glowing in the reproachful green eyes. 'If you go over there expecting to be able to do that, you're just setting yourself up for failure, and you're too intelligent for that. When you want to succeed at something you know you have to put your whole heart into it. Your mum and dad *need* you to be there for them, Beth. Don't disappoint them.'

'I don't have much choice, do I?' said Bethany stiltedly. 'If *you* don't want me...'

Rachel forced her voice to remain steady, although she felt clawings of panic shredding at her control. 'You have a choice about the way you behave—whether you accept with grace or try and make everyone around you feel guilty because life isn't perfect. You take your mum and dad's unconditional love and support for granted, but a lot of kids grow up without that kind of emotional security to back them up when things get rough.' Her eyes were clear as she picked her words carefully. 'I only wish your grandparents had been as protective of Robyn and I as Robyn and Simon are of *you*. It's difficult to have any confidence in yourself when you hear nothing but criticism and condemnation from the people you love...'

Bethany looked away, scuffing her thick-soled school

shoes on the tiled floor, the freckles standing out on her pale skin. 'I guess…' She lifted her chin and said with a totally false brightness, still avoiding Rachel's eyes, 'I suppose I'd better get my bag, or I'm going to miss my bus.'

Ignoring her half-eaten cereal on the table, she grabbed her lunchbox off the bench and rushed out of the kitchen. Rachel closed her eyes, letting out a ragged sigh as she sagged against the sink.

'Thanks.'

She opened her eyes to see her sister hovering in the doorway, her sweet face grave.

Rachel smiled wanly. 'For what?'

Robyn came into the kitchen, her eyes shadowed with relief and redolent with sympathy. 'For simply being an aunt.'

'You're my sister,' said Rachel. 'What else would I be?' They looked at each other, a world unspoken in the glance.

'She didn't really want to stay with me, anyway,' Rachel dismissed. 'It isn't a rejection of you and Simon. She's just temporarily got cold feet.'

'I know. But, still, if you'd given her the choice she was asking for it could have made things very difficult for us over the next few years.'

'Well,' said Rachel, 'I do have a pretty crammed life already. God knows I don't need the added complication of trying to cope alone with daily doses of teenage angst!'

Robyn wasn't fooled by her flippancy. 'Oh, Rachel, you would have got on famously, and you know it. If you were only thinking of yourself you would have said yes to her in a New York minute! I know you hated to hurt her, but she'll get over it. From what I heard she was trying to manipulate you with a sneaky form of emotional blackmail.'

So…she was the victim of two separate blackmail at-

tempts in one day, Rachel thought with an unexpected sting
of humour—and it was still only breakfast!

'Do you think she'll ever forgive me for letting her
down?' she couldn't help asking.

Robyn crossed to give her the hug she so badly needed.
'You haven't let her down. You love her and want the best
for her. You always have. She knows that.'

'I'm going to miss you all horribly,' she admitted gruffly.
Up until now she had been careful not to let them see how
shattered she had been by their decision to move abroad.

'I know.' Robyn responded to the rib-crushing fierceness
of her hug with a little gasp. 'But we're only going to be
an e-mail away, and at least I'll have plenty of spare time
to keep you up to date with our doings. We can even send
each other photos over the Internet!'

A short while later, when Robyn and Bethany had de-
parted for school and work, Rachel dragged the abused
package out of her handbag, grappling with the awful spec-
tre that her sister's innocent words had raised.

There were worse things than having yourself splashed
all over the tabloids. What if Matthew Riordan decided to
go global and posted those frightful pictures on the Internet!

She smoothed out his loathsome note and forced herself
to go over it again, word by horrible word.

In places the slashing green down-strokes almost seemed
to dig through the page, as if they'd been written in a rage.
Having seen the reputedly buttoned-down Riordan heir in
the raw, both literally and figuratively, Rachel could well
believe he was not as cold-blooded as his reputation made
out, but this outpouring of contempt made him sound dangerously reckless.

What did he really *mean* by his threats? They were actually rather vague. Should she wait for him to deliver more

specific demands…or was he assuming that she knew what they were?

Perhaps he intended to broadcast the photographs regardless of her response—or lack of it? How could she defend herself if he started sending copies to the press, to Westons' clients? Her family and close friends might believe her explanations, but to everyone else she would be reduced to an obscene joke. As Frank was constantly drilling into her, reputation was everything. He was so proud of the Westons name. If he found out that there was the slightest possibility of Rachel being involved in a scandal he would be furious. In order to protect the business she might well have to resign.

Rachel bit her lip, battening down her fear. She mustn't let herself be panicked into doing anything stupid. She should be thinking damage control, not capitulation.

She had heard Kevin Riordan boast that his son intended to run for City Council in this year's local body elections, with an eye to contesting the Mayoralty some time in the future. Logically, that meant Matthew Riordan had almost as much of a vested interest in keeping compromising photographs out of the public eye as Rachel did.

It was that *'almost'* which gave him his ruthless edge. He was prepared to subject himself to public humiliation and rely on his PR clout for damage control afterwards…but surely only as a last resort. At the moment the primary value of the photographs to him must be as a weapon to hang over her head.

All Rachel had to do was keep cool and try to exercise some damage control of her own.

If only she had known what she was getting into she would never have taken on the job of watching over Merrilyn Freeman's wretched dinner party!

CHAPTER THREE

'YOU'VE got to do something!'

Rachel jumped as Merrilyn glided up behind her and hissed urgently in her ear.

'About what?' Relaxed yet alert, Rachel thought everything was going swimmingly. A string quartet played exquisitely civilised Baroque on the terrace, the champagne was flowing, the caviare circulating, the conversation buzzing, and there had not been a hint of a problem with gatecrashers, light-fingered guests or suspiciously wandering staff.

Merrilyn's fingernails bit into her bare arm as she tugged her out of the way of a passing white-jacketed waiter. A slim redhead in an arresting green taffeta dress, she vibrated with nervous anxiety. 'He's going to ruin everything, I just know it!' she whispered frantically. 'I've spent months planning this! My first big formal dinner party and it's going to end up a total disaster!'

Rachel had been Merrilyn's fitness trainer for a year, and she was well acquainted with the young woman's propensity for worrying over trifles. The exclamation mark might have been invented with Merrilyn in mind.

'What on earth are you talking about?' she murmured soothingly, transferring her dangerously tilted champagne glass to her free hand. 'Everyone's having a great time.'

'I'm talking about *him*!'

Rachel followed her agonised gaze to the archway between the huge lounge and the sunken dining room, ex-

33

pecting to see some ill-bred, loutish interloper dipping his fingers into the caviare bowl.

'*Matthew Riordan?*' she said incredulously.

'Oh, God, just look at him…' Merrilyn moaned.

Rachel looked, ignoring the shivery frisson that lifted the fine hair on the back of her bare neck. She always instinctively bristled when she saw Matthew Riordan, and had learned not to take any notice of the uncomfortable sensation, which was normally a harbinger of trouble.

Viewed from the side, in formal black he looked leaner than usual, but otherwise impeccable, his knife-sharp profile tilted down as he poured champagne into the glass of a young society matron from a bottle which he had produced from under his arm. Whatever he was saying made her blush, and her middle-aged husband stiffen at her side.

'You see!' hissed Merrilyn, her nails stabbing at the nerve in Rachel's elbow. 'He's at it again.'

'At what?' asked Rachel reluctantly, easing her arm out of her clutches. She had done a sterling job of avoiding Matthew Riordan so far tonight, and would prefer to keep it that way.

'Saying wickedly provocative things to people.' She sounded on the verge of tears.

'Matthew Riordan?' Rachel said again, just to check that they were indeed discussing the same person. The man who was renowned for his cool reserve and deadly civility?

'Yes, Matthew Riordan,' moaned Merrilyn, her hand fluttering up to pluck at her diamond choker. 'Oh, God, John will never forgive me if he starts a *fight*—'

'Matthew *Riordan*?' gaped Rachel, beginning to feel like a maniacal parrot. 'For goodness' sake, Merrilyn, take a deep breath and *calm down*,' she said astringently. 'He's a merchant banker, not a lager lout. I've met the guy—he's intelligent and articulate, but abnormally controlled; I bet he knows exactly how far he can go.

'He would no more get into a stupid fight than he would pick up the wrong fork at dinner. He's certainly not going to insult his hostess or make a fool of himself by creating a scene. And none of your other guests are going to risk offending someone so influential—certainly not to his face.'

'You haven't heard the shocking things he's been saying!' Merrilyn despaired.

'Come on, Merrilyn. Give the guy a break.' Rachel couldn't believe that she was actually defending the man who was directly responsible for Weston Security Services losing two lucrative corporate contracts within the past month, but the important thing right now was to curb her client's hysteria. 'Everyone lets their hair down a bit at parties. Don't you *want* him to enjoy himself?'

'But he's *not* enjoying himself; that's the whole *point*!' Merrilyn's exquisitely made-up face was a mask of tragedy. 'He's *drunk*!'

Rachel almost laughed at the ludicrousness of the idea. 'I doubt it. He hasn't been here long enough to have had more than a couple of glasses of champagne—'

'No. You don't understand!' Merrilyn moaned. 'He was drunk when he *arrived*. And to think I was panicking because he hadn't turned up. Now I almost wish he *hadn't...*!'

The disgusted admission was tantamount to heresy from a dedicated social climber like Merrilyn, and Rachel registered a surge of alarm.

She reappraised him. 'He looks quite steady on his feet to me.'

'Trust me, he disguises it well, but he's on the brink of being bombed out of his skull,' said Merrilyn grimly. Once, on the massage table after one of their sessions in the gym, she had confided to Rachel that her brother was an alcoholic. 'And another thing—he's turned up solo! He was *supposed* be coming with Cheryl-Ann Harding. I've spent a fortune on the table settings—if his girlfriend's not here it's going to wreck the symmetry!'

'His *girlfriend*?' Rachel was startled. 'I thought he was married?' She had noticed the plain gold band he wore on his left hand.

'He *was*... Oh, hell, what's he going to do now?' Merrilyn was distracted by the sight of the ruffled young matron being hustled away by her stiff-jawed escort. 'If Cheryl-Ann isn't here he's going to be roaming around like a loose cannon all night,' she muttered. 'They've been going out for yonks—it's common knowledge that Matthew's father is putting on the pressure for him to get married again, and everyone agrees they'd make a perfect couple. If they've had an argument, why on earth couldn't they have saved it until *after* my party?'

She planted a hand in the small of Rachel's back, propelling her forward. 'Quick! Let's get over there while he's still by himself and see if you can keep him diverted long enough to sober him up for dinner.'

Rachel almost stumbled over her white slingbacks. *'Me?'*

'Well, that's why you're here, isn't it? To mix and mingle and stop minor problems escalating into major embarrassments?' declared Merrilyn. 'I can't tell you how much I appreciate you being here, Rachel. I'm so *glad* you persuaded me to go with Westons rather than some other firm. You're right, it's *so* much better having someone I *know* handling potentially sensitive matters like these. I'll be sure and tell all my friends what a classy personal protection service you run!'

Sensing she was overdoing the gushing flattery, she altered her tone to a panicky plea. 'Look, just stick to him like glue and do what you can to cover for him, OK? And be *discreet*! The fewer people who realise what's going on, the better.'

'Why don't you just politely ask him to leave?' murmured Rachel as they approached their target.

'Throw him out?' Are you *mad*?' Merrilyn's whisper was scandalised. 'He's one of my most important guests. It would be social suicide!'

She raised her voice on a fluttering laugh. 'Matthew! Look who I've brought to see you! I know I don't have to introduce you two—Rachel was just telling me she thinks you're the most intelligent and articulate man she's ever met!'

He had been topping up his own glass, and now he tucked the champagne bottle under the potted plant at his elbow with a casual disregard for his surroundings which made Rachel blink.

'Really? How delightfully flattering of her.'

He held out his hand, and although Rachel mistrusted his honeyed drawl, allied as it was with a mocking disbelief in the dark brown eyes, she automatically reciprocated. But instead of the cool, impersonal shake he had delivered when they had been first introduced to each other in his office, he raised her hand to his mouth and placed a string of tiny kisses across her long fingers, letting her feel the faint sting of his teeth.

'I shall endeavour to return the favour.' Bowed over her hand, his eyes were licensed to rove, and made the most of their freedom. 'Your breasts are truly in magnificent form this evening, Miss Blair,' he purred. 'What a pity they're so much more impressive than your IQ—but I suppose a woman can't have everything.'

Hearing Merrilyn's choked whimper of horror, Rachel gulped down her shock and pinned on a blinding smile.

'Can't she? What a woefully limited little world you must inhabit, Mr Riordan.'

His eyes flickered, the only indication that she had pinked him with her quick riposte.

'But I'm forgetting. One should never trust to appearances, particularly where women are concerned,' he continued smoothly, his gaze openly caressing the bounteous curves which plumped above the beaded edge of the gown. 'Perhaps it's your dressmaker or plastic surgeon who should be accepting my compliments...'

'With compliments like yours, who needs insults?' murmured Rachel, resisting the urge to hitch up her fitted bodice.

Merrilyn had shrieked with outrage when she had seen the subdued, off-the-rack black dress which Rachel had originally planned to wear.

'You can't wear that—it's not glamorous enough! You'll stand out like a sore thumb, which is exactly what we want to *avoid*. Give me your measurements and I'll arrange for my dressmaker to send over something more suitable.'

It had been Rachel's turn to be horrified when she had gone up to the bedroom where she was to change and found the strapless, figure-hugging sequinned dress hanging on the closet door. Unfortunately it fitted like the proverbial glove, giving her no excuse to demur.

'Oh, I do apologise...am I being insulting?' Matthew Riordan oozed with silky insincerity, making her stiffen as he twisted her wrist to rest his lips against her pulse-point.

By now Rachel could perfectly understand Merrilyn's panic. His diction was nearly perfect, but his words were stunningly uninhibited and his spectacles could not hide the hot, restless look in the hooded brown eyes. Apart from a streak of colour on his high cheekbones his face was noticeably pale in contrast to his sleeked-back hair and the dark stubble that graced his chin. His sultry air of controlled recklessness bore little resemblance to the grimly reserved chairman of Ayr Holdings whom Rachel had encountered when she had accompanied Frank to re-pitch for a couple of corporate contracts.

The companies, for whom they had run fraud prevention training programmes and provided security patrols, pre-employment vetting and confidential investigations in litigation support, had been involved in a series of mergers orchestrated by the majority shareholder—Ayr Holdings—and, having attained a controlling interest on several new boards, Matthew Riordan had been seeking to centralise their security arrangements.

At the meetings, although it had been made clear from the outset that Rachel was attending as co-owner of Weston Security Services, Matthew Riordan had virtually ignored her, addressing all his queries and remarks to Frank. When Rachel had taken it upon herself to answer or make an informed comment, he had given her minimal responses in a tone of clipped courtesy that had barely concealed his impatience with her interruption. Frank had claimed she was being over-sensitive, but Rachel had come away from their ultimately unsuccessful series of meetings steaming with frustration at being treated more like a glorified secretary than an equal partner.

'No, just unbelievably crass,' she replied, striving for just the right note of crushing boredom. She could feel his lips move against her skin as he smiled, the blood thumping through her artery his proof that she wasn't as calm as she looked. She tried to slip her hand free, but to her surprise she discovered his grasp was unexpectedly strong. A brief, almost invisible power struggle ensued, and Rachel finally resorted to the feminine trick of curling her angry fingers over the edge of his palm and digging her fake nails into the sinewy back of his hand. He didn't even flinch.

'What else did you expect?' he taunted. 'A woman like you wearing a dress like that...you're obviously not aiming to appeal to a man's *intellect*...'

Even though she knew full well she was being deliberately provoked Rachel couldn't help snapping at the bait. 'A woman like me?'

She had narrowed his hostility to a specific focus, and now she was paying the price. His smile was insolent in the extreme. 'Big, bold and brassy.'

The thin gold rim around her hazel irises glowed incandescently bright as she spluttered, *'Brassy—?'*

'It means flashy, strident, showy...' he elaborated, his eyes sliding from her breasts, heaving in outrage, to the tightness of her dress across her round hips and the slit in the side of the clinging skirt which revealed her leg to mid-thigh. 'I knew the first time you walked into my office what you really were—window-dressing...a showgirl trying to do a man's job...'

Rachel dug her fingernails deeper into his flesh and he gave an exaggerated wince.

'Uh, Rachel...' Merrilyn's voice fluttered anxiously to her ears and Rachel suddenly remembered the role she was supposed to be playing. She should be pacifying him, not prodding him into even worse behaviour.

She batted her eyelashes and adopted a girlishly meek tone. 'May I please have my hand back now, Mr Riordan?'

'It depends what you're planning to do with it,' he challenged, and she couldn't stop her eyes flickering to his temptingly exposed cheek. Unexpectedly he laughed, a purring sound that ruffled the nerves along her spine, and kissed her fingers again, releasing her hand with a slow, stroking motion that made it clear that it was purely his own choice.

'A toast,' he said, lifting his champagne glass and leaning forward to brush it against hers. 'To the unfair sex, who resort to seduction when all else fails.'

'If it was a man you would call it clever use of available resources,' Rachel responded tartly. 'And if you imagine this is a seduction you have some very odd opinions. You don't like women very much, do you, Mr Riordan?'

His eyes glittered darkly. 'I like *certain* women very much.'

'Let me guess...small, fluffy-headed, delicately built females who constantly defer to your superior intellect and would never dream of challenging your masculine superiority?'

His face tautened. 'What a sharp-tongued bitch you are!'

Her mouth curved smugly. She had obviously guessed right. She had probably just described Cheryl-Ann Harding to a T. She tossed back her champagne, forgetting that she had simply been holding it as a prop. 'Not your type, Mr Riordan?'

He looked her over, blatantly undressing her with his hot black eyes. 'I don't know—bedding you could have its... compensations,' he drawled insolently. 'As long as you kept your mouth shut. Except to scream at the appropriate moment, of course.'

'You mean the moment of my supreme disappointment?' she said sweetly, and had the pleasure of seeing his ears turn red. She could almost envisage the steam issuing forth. 'It must get very noisy in your bedroom, Mr Riordan.'

Merrilyn uttered a choked groan, overridden by Matthew Riordan's sneer. 'There's only one way for you to find out, isn't there?'

'Why, is this a proposal, sir?' Rachel simpered.

'Miss Blair, the *last* thing you'd ever get from me would be a marriage proposal,' he snarled.

'Good. Because being married to a chauvinist like you would make me feel suicidal!'

His face went stony-blank, his voice as vaporous as dry ice, and just as freezing as it bled from his pale lips. 'You wouldn't get the chance. I'd have murdered you beforehand. In fact, I'd be hard put to control my homicidal impulses until after the wedding!'

With that he yanked up the champagne bottle from under the plant and stalked off.

'Oh, God, oh, God, oh, God…' Merrilyn was chanting the horrified mantra under her breath, her face as white as milk under the professional coating of make-up.

'He insulted me first!' said Rachel shakily, knowing that it was no excuse. She had been thoroughly unprofessional. How many times had she heard David say that to successfully subdue a volatile opponent you had to remain emotionally detached from the situation?

'You don't understand…his first wife, Leigh, *did* commit suicide,' said Merrilyn. 'They'd only been married a few years…'

'Oh, *no*…' Rachel breathed. She closed her eyes, her own spiteful words ringing in her ears, lacerating her conscience.

'You've seen the kind of mood he was in, now he's going to be even *worse*,' Merrilyn fretted. 'I *told* you this was going to end up a disaster.'

'Look, don't worry, I'll handle it,' said Rachel, with far more confidence than she felt. 'I'll go and find him again—you just concentrate on looking after your other guests.'

'But we're sitting down to dinner soon! How can I concentrate on anything else? It'll be like having an unexploded bomb at the table!'

'Change the seating. I'm in a suitably obscure corner—put Matthew Riordan next to me.'

'After what just happened—are you kidding? That would really light his fuse!'

'There won't be any fireworks,' vowed Rachel grimly. 'If he won't co-operate I'll think of something else, but I won't let him create a disruption.'

To Rachel's relief Merrilyn appeared to accept her assurances although she still looked dubious as she hurried off to resume her hostessing duties.

Rachel didn't need a bloodhound to track down her quarry; all she had to do was follow the trail of nervous smiles and negative energy which Matthew Riordan had left scattered in his wake.

She found him outside, wandering down the terrace steps, having bypassed the glass dangling from his fingers in preference to swigging champagne straight from the bottle. The evening was so warm and humid that stepping from the air-conditioned comfort of the house into the velvety night was like being enveloped by a smothering blanket. The mingled scent of the jasmine which cloaked the walls of the large courtyard below the terrace and the Mexican orange blossom shrubs set in tubs around the kidney-shaped swimming pool was heavy in the air.

Approaching his brooding back as he prowled restlessly along the edge of the salt-water pool, Rachel decided that the grovelling approach would probably only invite his further contempt.

'Looking for a small dog or a child to kick?' she asked, and when he swung around to face her she didn't give him a chance to open his mouth.

'Don't you think you've had enough of that?' She nodded at the champagne bottle.

His mouth twisted, the lenses of his glasses reflecting the

dancing light from the flaming torches decorating the fluted columns in the courtyard.

'What are you? My conscience?'

'Since you apparently don't have one of your own, I felt constrained to volunteer,' she said acerbically.

'Like to live dangerously, do you?' He prowled back towards her, his voice thick with menace, but Rachel stood her ground. Let him know that she was far more than merely the sum of her curvaceous parts!

'Merrilyn's afraid that you're going to get totally smashed and run amok, insulting all her guests and ruining her chances of making it onto the social register.'

Her shrewdly judged frankness arrested the flaring animosity in his face. 'So she asked *you* to stop me?' he asked incredulously.

'Something like that.'

He took a long swallow of champagne and slowly licked his lips, taking one final step that brought him close enough for her to feel the heat from his body. 'You and whose army?'

Rachel jerked her eyes away from his mouth. It was a highly inconvenient time to notice that his lips were sensuously full, casting a sexy shadow over the intriguing indentation in his chin. 'I thought I'd start off by appealing to your better nature.'

'You're so sure I have one? It didn't sound as if you thought so back in there...' He jerked his head towards the partying buzz, tilting himself momentarily off balance before quickly adjusting his stance. A tiny slip but a betraying one.

'Back in there I was operating under a slight misapprehension,' she murmured.

He cocked his head. 'Oh, and what was that?'

'Merrilyn told me you were drunk, but I didn't believe her. I apologise for my stupid mistake.'

He gave a crack of reluctant laughter. 'You're taking a hell of a chance, aren't you?'

She didn't pretend to misunderstand. 'If you're going to take it out on anyone, take it out on me. Merrilyn issued her invitation in good faith. She wasn't to know that you'd have a tiff with your girlfriend and try and drown your sorrows.'

He paused with the bottle halfway to his mouth. 'Is that what she thinks happened?'

'Well, Cheryl-Ann's not here, and you are—distinctly the worse for wear, so...'

She watched him up-end the bottle again, her fingers itching to snatch it away from his lips. But she knew from their earlier encounter that he was a lot stronger than he looked, and stubborn as the devil. Cunning rather than brute force was the best way to handle him.

'Actually it was vice versa,' he said, catching her frustrated look and defiantly refilling his glass, toasting her with an exaggerated flourish before knocking it back.

'I beg your pardon?'

'It was *because* I'd been drinking that Cheryl-Ann refused to come along with me tonight...'

'Oh...' Rachel was disconcerted by his sudden revelation. Merrilyn had acted as if his behaviour was totally unprecedented, but perhaps he was a closet alcoholic.

'Cheryl-Ann likes everything in life to be pleasant and predictable. Particularly her men.'

'Are there so many of them?' she asked curiously. 'I thought you two were a big item.'

'And I thought you didn't believe everything Merrilyn tells you. More champagne?' he said, and splashed some into her glass from the carelessly offered bottle. Most of it slopped over the edge and onto her fingers.

'Sorry,' he said as she sucked in a gasp at the sudden chill. 'Would you like me to lick it off for you? No free hands.' He extended his arms wide in explanation, his unbuttoned jacket splitting wide over his snowy pleated shirt-front, now lightly frosted with bubbles.

'No, thank you,' she said primly, pushing away the unsettling thought of his tongue stroking across her skin. 'But if you'll hand me the bottle I'll pour myself some more— I don't trust your aim.'

He laughed again, and tucked the bottle under his arm. 'I may be drunk, but I'm not stupid.'

She shrugged. 'It was worth a try. You *could* be a bit more co-operative.'

'Why should I?' His mouth turned down, making him look wilful and determined to be difficult. She was reminded that while he seemed preternaturally mature, and commanded a lot of power in his position, exuding an air of intimidating and apparently effortless authority, he was still four years her junior. She should be able to handle him with one hand tied behind her back!

'Well, surely you don't want people to think that you're a lush?' she wheedled.

'I'm rich enough not to have to care what people think,' he said, with breathtaking arrogance and unfortunate accuracy. 'But, as it happens, I have none of the usual vices.'

'Just the unusual ones?' hazarded Rachel unwisely.

'What would you classify as unusual?' he murmured in a sultry undertone, his dark eyes suddenly uncomfortably curious. She was acutely aware of his closeness, and the restless energy that seethed through his body, creating an invisible charge that made her exposed skin feel supersensitive to the sultry air.

'Never mind,' she said hurriedly, running her hand nervously through her hair. At this rate she would soon be tearing it out! 'Look, can we just agree that you'll moderate your behaviour for Merrilyn's sake?'

'Not for yours? After all, you seem to be the only one willing to brave my drunken wrath. Why is that, by the way?' Cynicism coated his voice as he speculated. 'What's in this for you?' His eyes narrowed as he leapt from cynicism to suspicion. 'In fact, what are you doing here at all? Merrilyn's guests are all from the ranks of Auckland's social élite, the movers and shakers—on what grounds do *you* qualify?'

Rachel hesitated.

'I happen to be her personal trainer,' she said, but she had spoken a heartbeat too late. Even steeped in alcohol Matthew Riordan's brain was unnervingly quick.

'My God, could it be that you're not really here as a guest at all?' he murmured, with the beginnings of a goading smile. 'That you're just the hired help! I saw a car with Weston Security markings in the driveway—is that why you're here? Helping make sure that we movers and shakers aren't slyly pocketing the silverware?' He began to laugh, uninhibitedly.

'Could you please keep your voice down?' she snapped, looking over her shoulder at the people watching from the terrace.

His laughter abated to a taunting grin. 'I'm right, aren't I? You and that bulky young man on the door are playing on the same team.'

'WSS is supplying the security coverage here tonight, yes,' she admitted stiffly.

He rocked on his heels, shaking his head. 'I just don't believe it!'

Rachel had had enough of being the target for his amusement. 'What? That we're capable of doing a first-rate job? *You* may have chosen to think otherwise, but Westons has a string of very satisfied private and corporate clients who are extremely impressed with the services we deliver—'

'And what little service are you, *personally*, delivering this evening?' he wondered, with a mocking leer at her exposed skin. 'A "relief" massage for the stressed-out cat burglar?'

Even though she'd thought she was inured to sly jokes about being a masseuse, Rachel found herself blushing.

'I'm in charge!' she threw at him, and when his eyebrows climbed above the frames of his glasses she sucked in a furious breath at his provoking scepticism. 'You know damned well from reading our bids that I'm a qualified security guard—'

'With the ink barely dry on your certificate,' he charged.

'*And* a licensed private detective—'

'Ditto...both of which only serve to prove that you passed a police vetting of your background.'

'And in monitoring private functions like this, where there's a lot of valuable art on display and expensive jewellery around people's necks, it's standard practice to have operatives working undercover,' she finished grittily.

'Or, in your case, *un*covered!' he drawled, toasting her tight bodice with his glass. 'You've certainly perfected the art of distraction. With a *body*guard like you around, few men would be likely to find anything else worth pinching...'

'Is that why you stopped Westons winning those contracts we quoted on?' she burst out, the suspicion having haunted her ever since those abortive meetings. 'Not because we didn't present the best bid, but because of some stupid macho prejudice you have against *me*? Because of the way I *look* you presume I can't possibly be a competent professional. Is *that* why you've been whispering to your father and Neville Stiller, warning them against choosing us for the KR Industries job?'

'You think I'm *macho*?' His wandering attention was snagged by the diverting notion.

'Just answer the questions!' she rapped out.

'I thought they were rhetorical,' he responded blandly. 'In view of the sex discrimination act, if it *were* true I'd be stupid to admit to it...and we've both already agreed that I'm merely drunk.'

He crooked his elbow at her in a parody of politeness. 'I think I just heard the call to dinner. Shall we go in? No doubt Merrilyn's already arranged for us to sit cosily together, so that her pet Amazon can keep me firmly on the leash!'

CHAPTER FOUR

'I THINK a choke-chain would be more appropriate,' muttered Rachel as she reluctantly linked her arm with his. 'Are you going to behave during dinner?'

'Probably not...'

There was an angry bleakness in the laconic answer that made her heart sink. She halted, forcing him to swing around to face her, his back to the pool.

'Why?' She braced herself for yet another sarcastic, evasive response.

He shook off her hand and fortified himself with another mouthful of bubbles, uttering a sound of disgust when he discovered he had drained the bottle. He cast it with a reckless arm into the pool. It hit with a loud splash and bobbed briefly on the surface, then spiralled down through the ripples of light as the water poured in through the narrow neck.

He watched it sink with an intense fascination, waiting until the rippling surface of the water settled back into reflective smoothness before he spoke. 'You know...it was a night just like this; a perfect, romantic, cloudless, starry summer night...'

His lyrical tone gave Rachel an ominous tingling at the base of her skull. 'What night?'

'The night my wife killed herself,' he said casually, and Rachel's breath stopped in her throat.

'She—didn't...*drown*?' she stammered, alarmed by the fixed intensity with which he was staring into the pool.

He pivoted unsteadily on the coping stone to give her a

sardonic look. 'No, she wanted to make it neat and tidy for both of us. She took a handful of pills washed down with half a bottle of vodka...exactly four years ago tonight.'

Oh, God, no wonder he was in such a black fugue! On each anniversary of David's death Rachel, too, was a mass of raw nerves as she coped with the onslaught of painful memories, re-experiencing the angry sense of helplessness she had suffered at the time. But for Matthew the pain must be multiplied tenfold. At least Rachel had the comfort of knowing that the man she'd loved had died for a positive purpose—to save the life of the child his car had successfully swerved to avoid.

'Perhaps she expected to be found...' she offered tentatively, hampered by her ignorance.

'And saved? By me?' His laugh was bitter. 'Then I obviously failed her, didn't I? Her death was *my* fault...'

'That wasn't what I meant—'

'Even though she was married to *me*?' he lashed out. 'Grounds for suicide in itself. Wasn't that what you said?'

'When I said that, I didn't know about your wife—'

'You were just taking a lucky guess?'

She swallowed. 'I was angry. I was trying to think of the worst insult I possibly could.'

'Congratulations. You succeeded admirably!'

'Matthew, I'm sorry.' She reached out, unconsciously using his first name in an effort to re-establish their tenuous emotional connection.

He recoiled violently.

'Go to hell!' He struck her hand away and in that moment she knew that it would be sheer madness to let him sit down in polite company.

His self-control was too precarious. The alcohol had already stripped away far too many of his inhibitions, freeing him to express thoughts and feelings which would normally be taboo to a man of his pride and emotional reserve. He had gone beyond the point where he was willing, or even able, to exercise reasonable judgement.

Which meant that Rachel would have to fall back on her risky plan B.

While he was still swaying from the momentum of his action she surged forward with a little cry of alarm.

'Look out!' She caught his padded shoulders in a bunching grip. 'Don't move—' Her body bumped softly into his as he instinctively stiffened. '—or you'll trip over—'

He teetered on the brink of the pool as something firm slid against the back of his ankles, preventing him from shifting his feet to re-establish his centre of gravity over his arching back.

'The—' She snatched her hands back, her eyes flying wide with horror as he continued to topple backwards, his arms now windmilling wildly.

'Cat!' Her hands clapped over her mouth as he crashed down into the water, sending a small tidal wave spilling over the tiled edges.

'Oh, no!' she cried as the string quartet on the balcony craned to see what had happened in a cacophony of discordant strings. 'Matthew, are you all right?'

For one awful instant when he went under she thought he might not be able to swim, but he almost immediately resurfaced and began to swim clumsily towards the side, hampered by his waterlogged clothes.

'I could see it was going to happen but I couldn't do anything to stop it!' she cried apologetically.

A waiter and a few other guests hurried down the steps to assist, and she waited for them to reach her before she risked offering Matthew her helping hand. While one person falling in the pool could be dismissed as an accident, two would be serious grounds for gossip.

Merrilyn fluttered to the fore as he was hauled to his dripping feet. 'W-what *happened*?' she stammered.

'He tripped over the cat and fell into the pool,' Rachel told her succinctly.

Merrilyn's smooth brow wrinkled. 'But we don't have a—' She caught Rachel's eye. 'Oh, you must mean the *neighbour's* cat. That wretched tom is *always* prowling over here—one day I'm going to ring the SPCA...' She trailed off as Rachel's tight smile warned her not to overdo the descriptive colour.

'Unless I get my hands on it first and wring its damned neck!' growled Matthew Riordan, removing his fogged glasses and raking his hand over his wet head, sending little rivulets streaming down into the back of his collar. 'I didn't even see it!'

'It's coal-black,' Merrilyn said quickly. 'I'm most *frightfully* sorry, Matthew. How awful! *Naturally* we'll pay for dry-cleaning. Oh, dear, you're so *wet*!' she finished feebly.

'Water tends to do that to people,' he said blithely.

'And we were just about to sit down to our individual herb soufflés!' Merrilyn shrilled, clenching her beringed fingers over her heart.

There was a little pause, and Rachel could see her obsessive need to be the perfect hostess warring with her fervent desire be swiftly rid of her unexpectedly awkward guest.

There was an audible squelch as he shifted on his feet. 'Since I don't have my car with me, I can't drive home...and I can hardly get into a taxi like *this*,' he said impatiently, moving his arms and sending water cascading out of his sleeves.

Rachel noticed with alarm that his consonants were now definitely blurred and he was visibly unsteady on his feet. Instead of sobering him up, as she had half hoped, the adrenalin shock of his dunking had evidently speeded up the absorption of alcohol into his already saturated system.

'You can't let all those soufflés go flat, Merrilyn,' she said pointedly. 'Shall I show Matthew somewhere to dry off while the rest of you go ahead with dinner? Preferably somewhere that he doesn't have to trek back through the house—like your guest quarters, perhaps? He might like to have a shower, as well as a change of clothes...'

'Of *course*!' Merrilyn eagerly fell on the immediate solution to her dilemma. 'The guest-house would be perfect!' It was tucked well out of sight and sound of the main house. 'I'll send a maid along shortly with some suitable clothes.' But not shortly enough to interfere with dinner, she silently communicated as she added, 'Uh, do you need any help, Rachel...?'

Rachel had received the silent message. 'No thanks.' She wedged her shoulder discreetly under a dripping arm. 'I'm sure I can manage.'

'You will see that he has everything he needs?' Merrilyn couldn't help pleading.

'Of course I will,' said Rachel confidently.

She wasn't so sure of her ability to manage ten minutes later, as she was faced with the task of manhandling a fully-grown male out of his clinging wet clothes. Although Matthew Riordan had meekly allowed her to guide his listing body along the cobbled path around the house, once they had reached the guest-house he had turned infuriatingly passive.

'If you don't get out of those things soon you're going to get a chill,' Rachel repeated as he stood motionless in the middle of the big bedroom, creating a small puddle on the polished wooden floor.

He merely gazed at her blankly and she sighed, taking the spectacles out of his limp hand and placing them on the table beside the king-sized bed, with its wrought iron bedhead topped with shiny brass.

'Look, you're shivering already.' She put a hand on his chest to confirm her point and was taken aback at the heat burning through his wet shirt. Even given the warmth of the night it seemed unnatural, particularly in view of the visible tremors which were shaking his torso.

'I'm hot,' he said helpfully, and she moved her hand to lay it across his flushed forehead. That, too, felt uncomfortably warm. She frowned as he sighed and turned his face to rub it against her soft palm. 'Mmm...That feels so good...'

She flushed and hastily circled around behind him to collar his drenched jacket and ease it down his uncooperative arms. She carried it into the bathroom and dropped it into the expansive marble spa-bath. While she was there she turned on the pulsating shower in the transparent glass cabinet, hoping that the inviting sound would lure him in, but when she returned to the bedroom, carrying a towel with which to mop the water from the floor, he was still standing in exactly the same place, his bedraggled shirt hanging twisted and loose, his expression darkly frustrated.

'What's the matter?' she asked, averting her eyes from the drops of water sliding down his chest and pearling on his peaked brown nipples. She excused her momentary fascination as professional interest—his firm upper body suggested that he must work out, since he wouldn't retain that kind of muscle definition just sitting around in boardrooms.

'It won't come off,' he complained, plucking at the wet fabric on his shoulder.

'That's because you haven't undone your tie or cufflinks,' she said in exasperation.

Silk-shaded table lamps beside the rattan couch and the shiny brass bedhead had sprung to soft life when Rachel had keyed in the alarm code in the electronic panel by the door. Now, trying to read the expression in his eyes, she was sorry that she hadn't bothered to also flick on the overhead lights. Without the protection of his glasses his eyes seemed larger, their pale lids heavier, but in the muted shadows of the room it was impossible to guess what he was thinking as he stared at her with that strange, unblinking concentration.

'Matthew?'

'Matt. My friends call me Matt.'

'We're not friends, remember? We're practically strangers.'

'Rachel...'

At least he knew who she was, she thought humorously, and he didn't *sound* as if he bore a grudge...

Tossing the towel on the cream bedspread, she dealt briskly with the gold links in his sleeves and reached up to unsnap the studs which fastened the black tie. As she pulled it free from his wing collar his hands came up to settle heavily on her waist, and she stiffened as he swayed forward, his damp chest pressing against her breasts.

'What are you doing?'

'The room is moving,' he protested thickly, sliding his arms further around her body.

'It's not the room; it's your head,' she told him, pushing at his chest.

'It hurts.'

'What? Your head? Did you hit it when you fell?' Fears of delayed concussion swirled in her head. She ran her hands up the nape of his neck and sifted her fingers through the silky strands of wet hair, but could detect no flaws in the smooth symmetry of his skull.

'Not there,' he muttered, and took one of her hands and

pressed it back across his forehead. 'Yes, there...' He sighed with satisfaction. 'Your hands feel nice...so cool...'

In fact they were quite warm. He was running a slight fever, guessed Rachel. He wasn't only drunk, he was also ill. Which might explain why he was so *very* drunk.

'Are you taking any pills or painkillers?'

'Doctor says I don't need anything. Just mild flu. Hate pills. Never take them.' He shivered, his eyes closed, his voice hoarse. 'They don't kill pain, they cause it. That's how Leigh died. Too many damned pills!'

'So you were telling me,' she said cautiously, afraid his wife's name would be the trigger for another angry outburst.

'She shouldn't have done that,' he murmured. 'I loved her.'

'I'm sure you did,' she soothed. She noticed that the arm around her waist had relaxed and drifted southwards, his hand curving down the slope of her buttock, and hurriedly detached herself.

'You should be able to take off your shirt now,' she said, stepping back. She deliberately made her tone brusque, placing her hands on her hips to reinforce the distance she was consciously creating between them.

Unfortunately he appeared blind to the subtleties of her body language...but not to her body. His eyes dilated as they roved down the shimmering column of white sequins standing before him.

'I can't,' he said, in the same vague, unfocused voice. He shrugged helplessly, creating an intriguing interplay of muscle across his upper chest. *Trapezius, deltoid, pectoralis major, latissimus dorsi,* Rachel charted silently, forcing herself to see the biomechanical entity rather than an attractive man.

He was watching her from under his lashes, and she was

abruptly aware that, drunk or ill, he was still a consummate male. '*You* do it, Rachel.'

His suddenly sweet and beguiling smile made heat pool in the pit of her stomach. 'You haven't even *tried*.'

He pouted, and to her horror she found herself wondering what it would be like to suck on that sullen lip. 'I'm cold.'

She immediately felt a surge of guilt. What if his enforced swim had a further ill effect on his weakened immune system?

'You were hot only a minute ago,' she protested weakly.

He gave a dramatic shiver and she caved in, refusing to acknowledge the forbidden pleasure she took in removing his shirt, peeling the thin silk away from his damp body. His chest and upper arms were hard and smooth, the muscles twitching with tension as she picked up the thick peach-coloured towel and briskly blotted him down, trying not to notice the tingling in the tips of her fingers whenever they brushed his overheated skin.

As a masseuse, her sense of touch had become highly refined and her tactile skill made her very aware of the subtle changes in his body as his muscles began to relax. She instructed him to bend his head and vigorously attended to his hair, and when she moved around to deal with his back and shoulders he sighed with contentment, flexing his spinal column and rotating his shoulderblades, purring like a big cat.

'I like being rubbed,' he told her, his ability to communicate apparently reduced to simple expressions of sensory acknowledgement.

'Most people do. It stimulates the blood supply which in turn helps removes toxins at cellular level,' she said clinically, with a final dust down his lumbar vertebrae.

'It feels good, too,' he insisted, pulling the bunched towel back towards his abdomen, which was already perfectly dry. She let go of the plush folds and he staggered, the back of his knees hitting the edge of the bed. He sat down, letting the towel flop onto his squelchy shoes.

'For goodness' sake, you're going to make a watermark on the covers!' With a huff of annoyance Rachel knelt to slide his custom-made shoes off his feet and remove his wringing black socks. His feet were long and narrow, his toes straight and marvellously even. He wriggled them sensuously in her sequinned lap and she pushed them back to the floor, and sat back on her haunches, looking up at him expectantly.

He looked expectantly back, and she finally accepted the fact that he was so plastered that he wasn't going to do *any*thing for himself.

'Perhaps I should get a man to do this...' she said, even as she knew she wouldn't. There was something too elementally satisfying in having the man who was causing such strife at Weston Security virtually helpless in her hands. On a personal level there was an even more primitive response operating, one that Rachel didn't wish to dwell on too deeply.

He clenched his hands on his splayed knees, glowering at the suggestion. 'No—no one else. Only *you*.'

'You're the boss,' she said wryly, her conscience somewhat quieted by the arrogance of his plea.

His narrow white silk cummerbund had twisted on his hips when he had pulled out his shirt-tails, giving her easy access to the fastenings. Undoing the small silver hooks, she pulled it off and draped it over the edge of the brass bedhead, taking a deep breath as she reached out for the top of his trousers. Discovering the succession of tiny buttons was a shock, but she struggled on valiantly, even when it became obvious that the delicate bump and brush of her busy fingers was having an enlivening effect on his depressed nervous system. She heard him groan, and nearly leapt out of her skin when he cupped his hands on either side of her bowed head and began massaging the sensitive skin behind her ears with his thumbs.

'Matthew—'

His hands tightened on her scalp. 'Oh, Rachel…' He whispered a phrase that made her hasten hysterically to her task. Her fingers became more and more clumsy as they negotiated the changing contours of his lap, and as soon as the last button yielded to her feverish persuasion she scrambled to her feet and tugged off his sopping trousers with a final, punishing jerk that sent him sprawling back on the mattress.

His white designer briefs were moulded transparently to his form, and the sight of his still burgeoning arousal was indelibly printed on her brain in the few seconds that it took to scoop up the towel and toss it across his lap.

If she'd thought the most awkward part was over she was wrong, for, freed of the constriction of his clothes, Matthew experienced a burst of hyperactivity and decided that Merrilyn would be furious at them for missing her dinner. It took some fast talking, combined with body-blocking techniques learned from years of self-defence classes, to stop him from marching out of the guest-house, virtually *au naturel*, to deliver his apologies to the party at large.

Dismissing the shower as a practical impossibility, Rachel tried to convince him that he needed to lie down and rest while he waited for his change of clothes to arrive, hoping that once his head was on the pillow he might lapse into a natural stupor. She coaxed him back onto the bed by turning down the covers and slyly offering to give him a massage, but her cleverness backfired and turned into a physical tussle during which he became feverishly amorous.

She had figured that it would only take a few minutes of slow, gentle kneading for her to induce a sense of such physical well-being that he would doze off, and when she had informed him that he must lie absolutely still for his massage he had meekly lain back on the cool white sheets. But when she had knelt at his side and tried to get him to turn onto his stomach he had stubbornly refused.

'I want to watch,' he said huskily. 'I've never had a massage before.' He pulled her hand from under his shoulder and placed it on his chest, covering it with both of his as he pressed her fingers into the skin over his rapidly beating heart. 'What big hands you have,' he discovered in surprise, lifting his captured prize to inspect it.

Once upon a time such comments had used to hurt.

She gave her standard tart response. 'All the better to slap you with.'

His eyes sparkled darkly with innocent curiosity. 'Are you into spanking? Is that one of your "unusual vices"?'

His brain might be partially on hold, but there was evidently nothing wrong with his short-term memory.

'Certainly not!'

'Oh.' He had the nerve to sound slightly disappointed. 'Look,' he murmured, meshing their fingers together to measure their length. 'We're both the same size.'

'No, we're not,' she refuted. 'I'm taller, stronger and fitter than you are.'

But not smarter. His darting smile was the only warning she got before he pulled her sharply across his chest, sweeping one lean leg around the back of her knees and trapping her legs together within her narrow skirt as he rolled them both over until she was squashed beneath him, her hands pinned on either side of her head. She felt a brief shudder of sick panic as her mind slipped back into the distant past, and then her superb conditioning kicked in and they were rolling back and forth in a brief struggle for ascendancy.

Brief, because Rachel almost instantly realised that, whatever strength Matthew Riordan possessed, his stamina was sorely depleted and his alcohol-impaired motor skills made it simple to speedily counteract his clumsy moves. Never having wrestled with a semi-naked man before, she was seriously distracted by the slippery threshing of his limbs and the sinful pleasure that came from riding his squirming body, feeling all that latent male power quivering beneath her bare hands.

A dampness that had nothing to do with his fever bloomed on his skin, exuding a musky scent and belatedly making her realise that he wasn't fighting for victory so much as enjoying the arousing effects of a full body-to-body massage. The threat of physical harm, which had never been very real, was now eclipsed by a far more insidious menace.

'What on earth do you think you're doing?' she hissed as he slowly rotated his hips against the crush of her belly and uttered a sexy little moan.

'This is so fantastic...' he dreamed with closed eyes, his lower body undulating, his hand insinuating itself into the parted slit in her skirt, sliding up the back of her crooked leg towards the fullness of her bottom. 'You feel so different than I'd imagined...firm, yet so deliciously soft where you're most a woman...'

'Stop that!' she elbowed his arm away and straightened her leg with a jerk, and he groaned again as her knee dragged heavily across his swollen groin.

His hands moved over her sequinned back. 'Oh, yes...do that again. I like it when you're rough with me...'

'Matt!'

He opened his eyes and gave her a glazed smile. 'Are you going to take all your clothes off now, so we can have sex?'

The suggestion almost blew off the top of her head. *No!*

His sultry certainty didn't waver. 'When we're both nude I'll be able to feel every part of you against me…' His voice was thick with excitement 'Feel and see everything while we're making love—'

'We're *not* going to *be* making love!'

'Why?' He regarded her with heavy-lidded confusion. 'We're already in bed together—'

'We're *on* a bed, not in it,' she clarified. 'You're supposed to be resting—'

'But I don't want to rest. I want you to make love to me—'

To? Not *with*? Rachel's imagination ran riot even as she choked out, 'You can't always have what you want.'

'But you want it too,' he insisted. 'I know you do. I can *feel* it— I can see the way you look at me.'

He knew and felt and saw too damned much for a man who was supposed to be drunk and incapable!

It had been two years since she had experienced any sexual stirrings, and Rachel was unprepared for the sudden reawakening of her dormant feelings. She lashed herself with the knowledge that her carnal curiosity was shamefully inappropriate: he was too young; he wasn't in the full possession of his senses; he was, if not her enemy, then at the very least a serious opponent of her professional interests; and he was already involved with another woman. To succumb to his drunken seduction she would have to be both mad *and* bad…

'Stop it—Matthew, I'm serious! I don't want to have to hurt you,' she threatened, fending off his wandering hands.

'You won't hurt me…it's only women who sometimes find it painful,' he murmured bemusingly, his eyes hot and smoky. 'But I'm ready for you, Rachel. You can do whatever you like to me—I promise I'll like it.'

She felt a deep, erotic thrill. 'For God's sake, Matthew,' she whispered. 'You don't know what you're *doing*—'

'So? You can show me. Please…I'll be a good lover. I'm a very quick study and it won't take me long to figure out what you like best.' The phrases tumbled over one another, each word slurring into the next. He tried to slither clumsily on top of her, and in a flurry of sequins she pinned his back to the bed, hitching up her gown to straddle his hips with a pincer movement of her strong thighs, bracing herself above him on stiffened arms, her hands flat against his shoulders.

'I said *no!*'

'But Merrilyn told you to make sure I had everything I wanted,' he reminded her soulfully.

'She said *need*, not *want*.'

'But I *do* need you, Rachel.' His black eyes burned with passionate conviction. 'I need you *now*.' He dug his heels into the mattress and arched his hips, pushing himself up between her spread thighs in an attempt to demonstrate just how urgent was his desire. The swollen hardness barely contained by his damp underwear nudged at the gauzy lace covering the core of her feminine being, sending a secret tingle shooting along the cluster of exposed nerve-endings.

'You have to help me…you're the one she chose to soothe the savage beast.'

'Breast,' Rachel corrected automatically, and inwardly groaned at her stupidity as his steamy gaze obediently sank to her cleavage, brandished almost under his nose. 'It's savage breast, not beast,' she explained quickly. 'People often misquote that line.'

His mind did not appear to be improved by her informative little lecture.

'Your breasts don't look savage to me,' he told her gravely, his flattened hands creeping up her sides. 'They look like velvet pillows, all big and plush and soft.' He lifted his head from the pillow and drew in a deep, sighing breath. 'They smell nice, too...sweet and warm and spicy...'

His head sank back as his questing hands slid the final distance to cup the ripe fruit dangling so tantalisingly within his reach, cupping their overflowing weight in his hot palms. 'And they make an incredibly sexy handful...'

As Rachel looked down in shock he pressed a gentle, exploratory finger against one springy mound and watched in fascination as it sank deep into the creamy, resilient flesh. She sagged onto one arm, her biceps bulging with the effort of supporting her whole weight, and caught hold of his wrist in her strong fingers. 'Don't—'

'Why not? Don't you like me playing with them?' he asked huskily. 'I'll be very gentle...'

She felt a hot flush sweep over her body. 'Just keep your hands to yourself.'

The fingers of his other hand curled over the top of her gown. 'But I can *prove* that you like it...' He yanked down strongly and Rachel let out a little screech as a warm wash of air flowed across her freed breasts.

'I knew it was too low-cut for you to wear a bra,' he crowed smugly, shoving the tight bodice clear down to her tapered waist. 'See...your nipples are already excited.' He touched one ruffled raspberry peak. 'Would you like me to suck them?' he offered dreamily. 'I think I'd like to do that more than anything...'

Gasping at his audacity, and appalled by the sizzling temptation of his touch, Rachel reared up and gathered both his wrists in one hand, slamming them forcefully up over his head.

He laughed feverishly, treating it as a teasing new game, kicking his legs and bucking and twisting his body so that her breasts bounced against his sweaty chest. Desperate to control both him and the wayward desires still pulsing through her veins, Rachel snatched the cummerbund hanging from the shiny top rail of the bedhead and looped it tightly around his straining wrists, threading the free ends through one of the wrought-iron bars and securing it with a rough knot. As she did so her flushed breast brushed his cheek, and she felt his head turn and the hot, wet lash of his tongue…

Rachel's hands were shaking when she rolled off his body and dragged her bodice up to cover her sensitised breasts, shielding them from his regretful gaze. To her relief their final bout seemed to have left him weak and lethargic, and he made no attempt to escape from the bond which he could have quite easily pulled free with a little concentrated effort. Instead he lay quietly beneath the sheet that she tucked over him, following her around with his dark, brooding eyes until she agreed to release him on a vow of good behaviour.

He was still shivery, still feverish and disorientated, and Rachel managed to extract the name of his doctor from him and looked up the medical listings in the phone book by the bed.

Fortunately his physician was at home, and not so over-cautious or fee-conscious to think that a house-call to his wealthy patient was essential. He listened to Rachel describe the symptoms and cheerfully informed her that a short dousing was not going to turn a slight case of flu into galloping pneumonia.

'It's probably more the excess of alcohol he's suffering

from than anything else,' he said. 'Just make sure there's plenty of fluids on hand to counteract the dehydrating effects and let Matt sleep it off. He'll probably have a king-sized headache in the morning, but you can tell him from me that from the sound of it he deserves the hangover!'

Rachel had no intention of doing anything of the kind. Having always been the type to learn well from her mistakes, she waited only until he slipped into a restless doze before sneaking out to order one of the security guards to patrol his door. Then she breezed back to the party, bearing the convenient news of Matthew's medically confirmed illness with which to disarm the gossips.

She had basked in Merrilyn's profitable gratitude and had privately congratulated herself on her handling of an extremely tricky situation.

Until now.

CHAPTER FIVE

RACHEL flipped down the sun visor at the top of her windscreen and scrunched down behind the steering wheel as Matthew Riordan came down the steps from the restaurant, his lean body already at an impatient angle as he stepped onto the footpath.

She stuffed the remainder of her sandwich in her mouth and looked at her watch, noting the time in the spiral notebook lying open on the passenger's seat. Only half an hour for lunch, and a business lunch at that, she thought as she watched him briskly shake hands with the two business suits who were with him before striding off in the direction of his car.

For the past two days, ever since she had received his torrid threat, Rachel had been investigating her blackmailer, and amongst other things she had learned that he was not a man who liked to waste his time or energy on inessentials.

She watched him circle to the driver's side of his gleaming black Porsche, pausing to shrug off the jacket of his lightweight grey suit before sliding behind the wheel. She had been surprised when she had discovered the kind of car he drove. Somehow she had assumed that he would travel as his father did, in a chauffeur-driven limousine with a fax and a phone so that he could work while he travelled. But then, as she had already learnt to her cost, Matt Riordan was full of surprises.

In retrospect Rachel was extremely glad that she hadn't given in to her first impulse yesterday morning, which had been to storm straight over to his office and confront him with his moral depravity. As she had left the house and slammed her way angrily into her car she had been mentally composing a blistering lecture on his disgusting lack of ethics, vile cowardice and base ingratitude!

Then it had struck her that that was probably what he was *expecting* her to do...that he might be banking on provoking her into a panic reaction rather than a carefully considered response, and if she didn't go in extremely well armed for a fight then she could be setting herself up for another lesson in humiliation.

She had forced herself to calm down as she'd driven to work. She needed hard facts rather than wild theories before she decided what action it was safe to take. Whatever happened she had to keep a lid on things until Robyn and Bethany were safely gone.

She had still been debating whether to come clean with Frank as she'd parked her car and walked into the low-rise commercial building which Weston Security Services shared with a fax bureau and a firm of accountants.

'You're late,' had been his blunt words of welcome as she'd walked through the door, and she was instantly on the defensive.

'Things were a bit hectic at home,' she told him, regretting the unproductive half-hour she had spent simmering over the photographs, now stashed in her briefcase. She paused to greet Lannie, their receptionist, and accept a small pile of mail.

Frank frowned. With his stocky build, wheat-blond hair and blue eyes he sometimes reminded her joltingly of David, but he possessed little of David's personal warmth. Frank was an abrasive type A personality, who was driven, rather than inspired, to succeed.

'When you rang you said you'd be in by eight-thirty, so I arranged a debriefing on the Johnson insurance case.

Everyone else was on a tight schedule so we had to go ahead without you. I know your sister's leaving in a few days but we still have a business to run here,' he grunted.

'I'm sorry. It's just that something came up after I rang…'

She knew how much she owed Frank. He could have made it impossible for her to work alongside him, but although he had been originally reluctant, and had constantly tried to fob her off with make-work tasks, she felt he had grudgingly come around to accepting her right to the partnership.

'Are you sure you're OK to come back to work?'

'Just a bit of a headache,' she said, adjusting her nervous grip on her briefcase and its explosive contents.

Frank gave her a hard look. His naturally suspicious nature had made him a good detective, and as David's only surviving relative he had been very protective of his younger brother. He hadn't much liked Rachel when she and David had started dating, and even after they'd got engaged the relationship had never been particularly relaxed. Frank was divorced himself, toughened by his profession and cynical about marriage.

'If you're not well enough, you shouldn't be here.'

'I'm fine,' she insisted. Frank was so hard-bitten himself that he had little respect for the weakness of others. She hated it when he condescended to understand that she might not feel up to the job.

She decided in that instant that she wasn't going to tell Frank about her humiliating problem—not while there was any chance she could quietly handle it herself.

'OK, that's good, because we have a major problem looming,' said Frank, following her into her small sunny office.

'What kind of problem?'

'Matthew Riordan!'

'W-what?' Rachel's briefcase slipped from her nerveless hand and crashed against the side of a filing cabinet. 'Why? What's he done now?' she asked with brittle casualness.

'It's not what he's *done*, it's what he's *going* to do,' fumed Frank. 'His father's had a heart attack.'

'Kevin Riordan?' Rachel was genuinely upset. She had liked the brash and ebullient head of KR Industries, who had shown a flattering admiration for 'feisty' women. He had been a welcome surprise after his infuriating son. 'When? Is he all right?'

'Keeled over at his desk on Monday. All I know is that he's in hospital and likely to be there for a while.'

'Oh, no, how *awful…*' she said, thinking of his boastful plans for an energetic retirement. 'He isn't even sixty-five yet…'

'Yeah—awful for *us*.' Frank dismissed her unselfish concern with a scowl. 'Because Matthew Riordan's stepped in to effectively run KR Industries, just when our fraud prevention package is on the table for a final decision, and so far he's got a one hundred percent kill-rate on our deals!'

Rachel was confused. 'But—I thought he had no official standing at KR—surely Neville—'

'Neville is away in Japan—I got a fax from him last night,' Frank said, drumming stubby fingers on top of the filing cabinet. 'He'll obviously take over when he gets back, but at the moment he's out of the loop. With him pushing our case the old man was bound to have approved our bid, now with Junior minding the store we might not get it signed by the deadline. That would mean having to go through the bid process all over again.'

'But Matt Riordan's not going to make any major decisions if he knows he's only keeping the chair warm.'

Frank's paranoia was running rife. 'Don't you believe it.

Neville told me that he doesn't trust the bastard an inch. If Riordan has overall power of attorney for his father he can virtually do whatever the hell he likes. With his position and influence he could do a lot of damage in a few days. I wouldn't put it past him to try to sabotage our bid…'

Rachel thought of the contents of her briefcase and felt her stomach lurch as Frank plunged on. 'I think we need to face the fact we may not be able to make that balloon payment after all…'

'I could mortgage the townhouse—'

'No!' Frank rejected the offer as forcefully as he always had before. 'David gave that to you free and clear and it's going to stay that way. Anyway, it would put your equity in the company at more than the whole is worth right now. If the worst comes to the worst we can maybe try downsizing, or even selling our client base…

'We have to be realistic, Rachel,' Frank told her. 'We were banking on that KR contract coming through and without it our chances don't look good. I'll sort through our options and try and figure out something, and, in the meantime, why don't you do some personal digging around on Riordan himself? See if you can come up with anything that might be useful.'

His tone doubted that she would. If he had seriously believed that an investigation was likely to be productive he would have put one of their senior men on the job, but unknowingly Frank had provided Rachel with the perfect excuse to devote the rest of the next few days to stalking her prey and plotting his downfall.

Wanting to make the most of her fast-dwindling time with Robyn and Bethany, she had used her illness as an excuse to cancel the rest of the week's gym appointments and several massage bookings at the physiotherapy clinic, so she had no other demands on her time until the following Monday.

Now, Rachel softly depressed the accelerator, rolling her car slowly forwards past the row of parked cars as Matt Riordan began to ease his Porsche out of his parking space further down the road.

She pulled down her baseball cap and adjusted her sunglasses. She didn't know exactly what she expected to achieve by tailing him around, but it was better than doing nothing. David had always believed that dry fact-gathering was no replacement for personal observation when trying to guess what a suspect's next move might be.

After spending all of the previous day delving into the microfiche files of old newspapers at the central library, checking property and legal records and making numerous phone calls under a variety of names, Rachel had been chafing to take some *real* action.

After calling to check that he was still in the building, she had driven over to KR Industries head office and waited until dusk in order to find out which of the three Riordan-owned Auckland properties Matthew was currently calling home. If it did come down to forcing a confrontation, she'd rather it was well away from the public eye.

His destination had turned out to be not his own city apartment, but the family's three-storeyed modern mansion on Auckland's millionaires' mile. Rachel had followed the black Porsche's tail-lights through the city streets, careful to change lanes irregularly and hang one or two cars back, and had felt a little thrill of triumph when she'd seen Matt Riordan finally swing in through the electronically operated iron gates which guarded the estate, still unaware of her presence. Her hands had been sweaty on the steering wheel and her heart had fluttered with exhilaration as she'd continued on past and parked further up the street, in the inky shadows of an overhanging pohutukawa tree, and savoured the small victory—her first solo tailing job!

Using her company cellphone, she'd checked her voice messages, then rung Robyn to let her know that she was on her way home. As she'd been saying goodbye she was startled to see the gates reopen and the black Porsche sweep out again and purr off into the night. He must have only called in to drop something off or say hello to his mother, she'd thought in dismay.

By the time she had got her engine restarted and fumbled her gears it had disappeared around the corner, and at the next intersection it had been only a wink of a brake-light at a distant curve, heading back towards the city. Rachel had pursued the streak of black metallic paint pulsing under the orange street lights on the straight stretch ahead as fast as she'd dared, and had actually believed she was catching up when she'd been flagged down by a uniformed police officer standing by her unmarked car, and handed the indignity of a speeding ticket and an on-the-spot breath test.

'What about that Porsche ahead of me? He was going just as fast—why didn't you stop him?' she'd complained.

'Because he had the sense to slow down as soon as he spotted me and not register over the speed limit on my radar,' the female officer had said drily.

Flushed with annoyance, Rachel had tucked the ticket in her notebook and set off again at a sedate pace, resigned to the fact that she had no chance of catching up with her quarry. She had driven past Matthew's apartment building, noting the darkened windows of his top floor corner eyrie, and vowed not to be taken off guard so easily the next day.

Now, pulling into the heavy lunchtime traffic behind the gleaming Porsche, Rachel thought that at least there would be no chance of breaking the speed limit today!

Expecting him to head to another business meeting, or

go back to the office, she was intrigued when he turned off towards a leafy suburb—until she remembered that it was where the city's newest private hospital was located. She had looked it up in the telephone book the previous day when she had wanted to find out Kevin Riordan's medical condition.

Rachel drove into the open car park and surfed into an empty spot on the waves of heat which shimmered off the surface of the new black seal. She nibbled on her lower lip as she watched Matthew lock his leather briefcase into the boot of his car and shoulder back into his jacket as he made for the double glass doors of the hospital. What she wouldn't give to be able to rifle through the contents of that briefcase!

A thick-set uniformed security guard—unfortunately not one of Westons'—was strolling between the cars, and Rachel thought he might think it suspicious if she remained lurking in her car rather than seeking the air-conditioned coolness of the hospital. Besides, a comfort stop was a growing imperative. Rachel was already suffering from sitting for too long in a small metal box under the blazing sun. Her short-sleeved silk tunic top was sticking to her back, and while the car was stationary the fan blowing air around her sweeping skirts was merely recycling the oppressive heat.

The hospital looked big enough and busy enough to provide plenty of cover, she reasoned. Perhaps she might even manage a quick snoop to find out how Kevin Riordan was *really* doing behind the smokescreen of official information. Taking a charitable view, maybe it was the stress and worry over his father that had caused Matthew to flip out. Maybe he had stooped to a sordid act of blackmail while the balance of his mind was disturbed?

She shivered in spite of the oppressive heat. Those had

been very the words quoted in a news clipping about twenty-four-year-old Leigh Riordan's tragic death. Most of the details had been suppressed, but not the coroner's final decision—that she had taken her own life 'while the balance of her mind was disturbed'.

But, no, she told herself, the charitable view was difficult to take when the fact was that Matthew had had those sleazy photos taken over a week *prior* to his father's heart attack.

The coronary care wards were on the third floor, and, unwilling to risk being caught in a lift, Rachel ran lightly up the stairs, two at a time, blessing her rapid return to fitness. She wasn't even breathing hard as she peeped around the heavy smoke-stop door on the third floor, reassured by the evidence that lunchtime was a popular visiting hour. Opposite her was a spacious dayroom peopled with a mix of elegantly dressed visitors and bathrobe-attired patients.

Halfway down the polished corridor she could see a T-intersection, where the nurses' station was situated, and more people moving about—the staff distinguishable only by the open white coats they wore over their smart clothes. In her thigh-length sand-coloured tunic worn over her filmy, patterned brown skirt Rachel was confident of blending in.

A logo on a door across the way caught her eye and she darted for the women's restroom with a sigh of relief. While she was in there she took her plastic pump bottle out of her capacious shoulder-bag and refilled it from a filtered water dispenser, and spritzed a dash of refreshing cologne across her throat and wrists.

Replacing her sunglasses, she cautiously exited and walked towards the nurses' station, her eyes flicking over the patients' names posted outside the individual private rooms.

She had almost reached the intersection when she glimpsed a grey suit around the corner of the right-angled reception desk and shied backwards. At the same time that she realised the suit-wearer was a woman, her reversing heel ground down on something soft and uneven.

Her cry of dismay mingled with a similar one of pain as she lurched around, her sunglasses tumbling off her nose to join the cascade of envelopes and the bunch of flowers which her swinging shoulder-bag had knocked out of the clutches of the tiny grey-haired woman woefully flexing one crushed foot.

'I'm most dreadfully sorry. That was entirely my fault. Are you all right?' Rachel burst out, thanking the Lord that she was wearing flat sandals. From her pain-creased features, Rachel judged the woman to be somewhere in her mid-sixties and, knowing how brittle older bones could be, she crouched to inspect the damage, relieved to see only a faint impression of her sole on the reddened top of her victim's foot.

'It looks like you'll just have some bruising. I'm *so* sorry; I know how painful something like that can feel!'

She hastily gathered up her sunglasses, scrabbling together the scattered mail and injured flowers before rising back to her full height. The other woman couldn't have been much more than five feet tall, and Rachel immediately felt like a clumsy giant as she loomed over the tiny figure in the fashionable powder-blue summer suit.

'It's really not that bad,' said the lady bravely. 'And it couldn't have happened in a more convenient place, could it?' She tested her foot gingerly back on the ground and smiled kindly at her sheepish assailant. 'Are you on the staff?'

'Oh, no—I don't work here,' Rachel responded with a weak smile. 'I don't think the hospital would be too keen to employ someone who goes around trampling people down!'

'I don't know—you could generate them some very brisk business.' The woman laughed. Although she was expensively dressed, and the triple strand of pearls around her neck undoubtedly genuine, the vibrant Kiwi twang in her accent bespoke down-to-earth origins.

'Or get them sued *out* of business. I'm afraid your flowers may be a little bit bruised, too.' Rachel smiled apologetically as she handed them back.

'Oh, well, I don't suppose my husband will notice. He'll be too busy complaining I haven't brought him whisky and chocolates.'

Rachel was amused by her expression of loving exasperation. 'In a coronary care unit?'

'He's a very bad patient,' the little lady admitted ruefully. 'He's always been so proud of being as tough as old boots—never had a sick day in his life until this...'

'Is he *very* ill?' Rachel asked warily.

'He had a heart attack, but they've decided it's not his heart that's really the problem—so now they've scheduled him for a triple by-pass.' An age-spotted hand worried with her pearls. 'The surgeon says it's very straightforward nowadays...'

'I'm sure your husband's in the very best of hands,' reassured Rachel firmly. 'Is your family visiting with you?' she asked, beginning to hand over the thick wad of cards and letters she had picked up, waiting patiently as the woman sorted them to fit them in her grasp.

'Well, my son was supposed to meet me here,' the woman confided. 'But he probably arrived early in order to interrogate the doctors to within an inch of their lives and order them not to upset his sweet little old mum by going into too much gruesome detail—never mind that I'd prefer to know everything there is to know. He's a lovely boy, really, but he can be so very *managing*...'

Her irritation showed and Rachel grinned. 'I know the type.'

'But you're so wonderfully *tall*,' admired the older woman, making herself an instant friend for life. 'I wish I was like you. I always get a crick in my neck when I have to argue with my husband or my son. It must be lovely to be able to stand up to bossy men and look them straight in the eye.'

'Or, better still, look down on them,' grinned Rachel.

She found herself on the receiving end of an assessing look as the grey head cocked to one side, soft curls framing the still-pretty face. 'You might be taller than my boy, but not by much...'

Rachel answered the silent question. 'I'm a hair off six foot.'

'Ahh. So you'd have almost a whole inch with which to lord it over my son. He doesn't seem to have cottoned onto the fact that we're really the superior sex. Mind you, that's partly my fault—he was a late baby, you see, and an only child, so he was doubly spoiled. I wasn't in the best of health for a while, so that probably encouraged him to re-gard women as generally rather fragile beings. Then his father insisted he be sent off to boarding school to toughen him up and acquire the correct degree of polish.' She sighed. 'Unfortunately I think it succeeded *too* well. He was a passionate, sensitive little boy who became a rather in-troverted adult. He had one or two bad experiences with women—he married once, when he was twenty, but it came to a wretched end—so now he seems to reserve all his passion for his work...'

Rachel was getting a very bad feeling. Her eyes fell to the last envelope she was in the act of passing over—a thin foolscap rectangle whose neatly typed address jumped out and hit her in the face.

Her fingers unconsciously tightened on the envelope, preventing it from leaving her hold as she blurted, 'You're Mrs *Riordan*. Mrs *Kevin* Riordan?'

'Why, yes—I'm Dorothy...do you know my husband?'

Of all the ghastly coincidences!

'Only slightly. My firm has quoted for some business with him. When I heard yesterday that he was ill I rang the hospital to see how he was but all they would tell me was that he was in a stable condition.' Rachel heard herself babbling while her brain screamed at her to get out of there as fast as she could!

'And now you've come down to make a personal enquiry?' Dorothy Riordan's small face lit from within. 'That *is* kind of you. Kevin's not having visitors yet, but I'll tell him you called, Miss...?'

As Rachel dithered over whether to lie a cool voice denied her the chance.

'Blair. Rachel Theodora Blair.' A grey-clad arm reached between them and plucked the envelope out of her white-knuckled hand. 'Thank you, Rachel, I'll take that!'

Rachel spun around to stare in guilty horror at the man who had prowled silently up behind her. There was a muted fury in the chocolate-brown eyes as he looked from the envelope in his hand to her stricken face.

'Oh, Matt, there you are!' said his mother happily. 'Do you know Miss Blair, too?'

Matthew showed his teeth. 'Intimately.'

His mother looked startled at the throaty purr, and Rachel flushed, edging back as he deliberately invaded her personal space.

'She was just telling me she's come to see how your dad is...'

'Was she?' Matthew's cynical murmur made Rachel scramble to correct Mrs Riordan's flattering misconception.

'Actually, I'm—I was—'

'Making a special delivery?' Matthew suggested, saluting her with a taunting flick of the envelope now in his possession. In the austere grey suit and plain blue shirt and tie he presented a picture of civilised menace that made her nerves twitch.

'Just passing...' she finished lamely, casting Mrs Riordan an unconsciously pleading look.

'I've brought all the morning mail from home, Matt.' His mother showed him the rest of the collection in her hand. 'I thought it might give your dad a nice boost to see some of the cards and letters that people have sent, wishing him well.'

'Is that what this is, Rachel?' asked Matthew silkily, turning over the envelope in his manicured hands. 'Greetings from a fond well-wisher?'

'I have no idea,' she said, grateful for his mother's restraining presence.

Her gratitude was premature.

'Really? I thought you were a woman who liked to always be *on top* of everything,' he said in that same low drawl. 'A lady who prefers to be in a *controlling* position in all her dealings—holding the *whip hand* over the rest of us, so to speak...'

Rachel glared levelly at him, her firm jaw clamped shut to contain her outrage. He was blatantly admitting it! He was virtually *boasting* about what he had done, in front of his own mother!

Thankfully Mrs Riordan was looking curious but unenlightened by his innuendo-laden comments.

'Goodness, it sounds positively frightening,' she said innocently. 'What is it you do, exactly, Miss Blair?'

Rachel told her about Weston Security. Trying to keep her attention on the conversation was extremely difficult with Matthew subtly crowding her on the physical as well as psychological front. Her skin goose-pimpled where the polished fabric of his jacket sleeve brushed her bare arm too often for it to be accidental, and if she turned her head even slightly in his direction her senses swam with a heady masculine scent which struck a disturbing chord in her memory.

'How fascinating! It must be a very exciting field.' Mrs Riordan's enthusiasm had the ring of genuine interest. 'I suppose you need a lot of experience?'

'Oh, Rachel is a highly experienced woman,' supplied Matthew laconically. 'She omitted to tell you that she also works as a masseuse, and I can personally testify that she's *extremely* exciting in the field!'

This piece of loaded sexual innuendo did not slip by unnoticed. 'Matt!' His mother's pained surprise was a parental rap across the knuckles.

'It's all right, Mrs Riordan.' Rachel seized the chance to get some of her own back. 'I'd already come to the conclusion before today that your son wasn't spanked enough as a child.'

His eyebrows rose above the wafer-thin tortoiseshell frames. 'Are you offering to put me over your knee, Mistress Blair?'

'Matt!'

This time they both ignored his mother's faint protest.

'It would be a wasted effort—you're obviously beyond any hope of redemption,' snapped Rachel.

'Is there ever any redemption to be gained through vio-

lence? And isn't spanking considered a form of child abuse
these days? Some mother *you'd* make...'

Her eyes became molten pools of gold as his casual
thrust penetrated deep into her guarded heart. Her hands
and feet felt icy while her head swam.

I'd make a *wonderful* mother, she wanted to scream back
at him. I *did* make a wonderful mother... I did everything
that a mother is supposed to do for her baby—suffered the
pain, made the sacrifices, and created something supremely
good out of a nightmare of hatred and fear...

Shaken by the wounding ease with which he had pierced
her defences, Rachel smothered the painful gush of bitter
memories and lifted her chin, offering him a sullen, stoic
stare so different from her usual antagonistic challenge that
his expression sharpened with predatory interest.

'Mum, why don't you take those letters along to show
Dad?' he said suddenly, not taking his eyes off Rachel's
pale mask of self-control. 'The cardiac surgeon is still with
him, so you can ask him all the questions we were talking
about last night...'

Was *this* where he had been off to the previous evening?
Rachel lacerated herself for overlooking the obvious. Some
detective *she* was!

'Are you ordering me to run along?' Mrs Riordan's wry
question showed that she was no fool.

Matthew turned a sweet smile on his mother that made
Rachel catch her breath. This was Mrs Riordan's 'sensitive
little boy' in the full glory of his maturity. 'Would you
mind? I've already had a good chat to Dad. Rachel is too
shy to admit it, but she's actually here to see *me*...'

'Oh?' Dorothy Riordan raised pale, pencilled eyebrows.

'Yes, she and I have some...' He paused delicately, sliding his hand down Rachel's forearm and entwining his
warm fingers firmly with hers, stiffening his arm in order

to hold them shoulder to shoulder as he looked into her flaring eyes. 'Unfinished business…'

'Oh, I *see*…'

'What did you have to say it like that for?' Rachel rounded on him as soon as his mother was out of earshot. 'You know what she thinks now, don't you?'

'That we have some business to conduct?'

'The only business implied by that suggestive little act of yours is *monkey* business!' she snapped.

'Better she thinks that than realises the truth,' he returned with a bite. Jerking her by the hand, he began marching her back down the corridor.

'What *truth*?' Rachel scorned to fight his hold, defiantly matching him stride for stride.

'That you're willing to risk my father's life to make a cheap score!'

'*What?*'

He suddenly stopped, pushed open a door that was slightly ajar and nudged her into a small room lined with crowded shelves. So distracted was she by his outrageous claim that she didn't realise what was happening until it was too late.

'What do you think you're *doing*?' she screeched as he kicked the door shut behind them. Her shoulder bumped against a shelf of folded sheets as she hastily tried to widen the distance between them in the narrowly confined space. The overhead light threw Matthew's grim face into harsh relief as she protested shrilly, 'This is a supply cupboard!'

'I stand in awe of your powers of deduction,' he sneered, leaning back against the door as he tore open the envelope in his hand.

'That was addressed to your father, not you!' she accused.

'And what is it you're so keen for him to see? Ahh, what

have we here? Another episode of the *Lifestyles of the Sick and Shameless*?' He flashed her a familiar set of images and she sucked in an appalled breath.

'Oh, my God!' She raised her bewildered gaze to his.

'You bitch!' He exploded away from the door. 'You had to keep turning the screws, didn't you? Even when you knew it wasn't going to get you what you wanted!'

She cracked her elbow on a ledge as he backed her into the nest of shelves in the corner. 'I don't know what you're talking about!'

He brandished the photographs under her nose. 'You were trying to foist these on a sick man—'

She shook her head in confusion. 'I *wasn't*—'

'The hell you weren't!' He slammed his hands flat down on the shelves on either side of her hips, his breath hot on her face. 'I *saw* you handing them to Mum. If I hadn't stopped you she'd probably have taken them in and opened them in front of Dad.'

'But I had nothing to do with those.'

His eyes flamed behind their twin shields of precision glass. 'So you're a liar as well as being malicious!'

The slap resounded as a sharp echo in the small room and Rachel watched in awful fascination as the white outline of her palm on his lean cheek filled up with blood. For a moment there was no sound but their mutually quickened breathing.

'You looking to get physical with me?' he growled, leaning closer.

In the space between one heartbeat and the next his anger ripened into a different kind of passion.

'I thought you only did that with men who were tied down...'

Rachel's body throbbed in recognition of his excitement, her skin drawing tight over her flesh, her breasts aching with the memory of what it felt like to be fondled in his eager hands. She remembered the smooth glide of his glossy skin, the hard flex of his muscles, the soft abrasion of hair on his thighs, the way his hips had surged between her spread legs. A soft, liquid warmth burst inside her belly and she shuddered.

'Take your hands off me!'

'I'm not touching you,' he pointed out hoarsely, and she realised to her mortification that it was true. The tension that had underpinned their every encounter was suddenly laid starkly bare.

She flushed.

'How dare you get all self-righteous with me?' she panted. '*You* were the one who opened up this particular Pandora's box. You can't blame *me* if the evils you let loose have come back to haunt you!'

He was studying her mouth as it moved, and she knew from the sultry, bitter-chocolate gaze that it wasn't her words in which he was interested.

'The only thing that's been haunting me is you,' he murmured. 'The memory of the touch and taste and smell of you...so real and yet so elusive. If it wasn't for the pictures I might have believed it was all some wild dream...like the ones that I've been having nightly ever since...'

His meaning sank like warm honey into her bones. She thought of all the nights that she had woken, hot and sweaty, from a faceless demon lover's embrace; but faceless only because she had resolutely refused to see.

'Stop looking at me like that!' she demanded weakly, her bag sliding unnoticed off her shoulder to slump limply to the floor.

'Like what?'

She turned her head aside from the erotic intensity of his stare and felt his breath moist in her ear, feathering up into her hair as he leaned even closer, his legs crowding against hers, his tie sliding against the front of her tunic, settling lightly between her breasts. 'Like what, Rachel? Tell me...how do I look at you?' he asked as she tried to hold herself rigidly aloof from the tumult of fire in her blood.

He nuzzled at the point of her jaw just below her ear and licked a hot trail back up to her soft lobe.

'How do I look? As if I want to eat you?' He nipped at the succulent flesh, keeping it captive between his teeth as she arched her neck away, then releasing it to press his open mouth into the sensitive hollow between the stem of her neck and her collarbone and drink in the taste and texture of her skin. 'That's because I do! God, how can someone so bad taste so damned good...?' he groaned.

Since she was fifteen Rachel's worst nightmare had been to find herself pinned down by superior strength, trapped and helpless against a greedy male assault. But where was the revulsion, the fear and the fury to defend herself now? She was rendered helpless—not by the violence of *Matthew's* sexual need, but the uncontrollable desires that raced recklessly through her *own* veins.

Her hands, which should have been groping for a way to swiftly incapacitate him, were instead sliding around his waist underneath his jacket, her arms slowly contracting until her breasts were crushing satisfyingly tight against his crisp cotton shirt-front. Her knee, which should have been aimed in a punishing jab between his legs, was instead obeying a more primal instinct, slowly rubbing up and down the outside of his thigh as he worked his lower torso deeper into the fork of her body.

His hair, soft and fragrant with natural musk, brushed her nose and cheek as his marauding mouth strayed over her throat, her chin, her cheekbones, her eyes, everywhere but where she desperately wanted it to be... Reason spun beyond her reach as she relinquished her fragile grasp on reality and cast herself adrift on a storm-tossed sea of pure emotion.

'Matt...' She tunnelled her hands up between his shoulder blades and raked her trim nails all the way down the length of his back, hard enough for him to feel the sharp scrape through the polished cotton.

He arched and shuddered, sensation pooling at the base of his spine and spilling over into his loins. 'Witch...!' His hands, which had been gripping the edges of the shelf in a futile attempt at self-control, swooped down to her flanks, smoothing up her thighs and over her womanly hips, tracing the rounded shape of her full bottom through the filmy skirt, snagging his fingers in the soft gathers as he kneaded her against his growing hardness.

Thready gasps mingled with whispered sighs and the rustle of cloth as their mutual excitement exploded into hungry passion. And still he had not kissed her...!

Matthew's rough-shaven jaw rasped tantalisingly across Rachel's soft lips, and with a stifled sound of frustration she clenched her hands in his thick dark hair, holding his head still so that she could at last find the intimacy that she craved. He resisted only long enough to wrench off his spectacles and shove them blindly into his jacket pocket, then his mouth was settling hotly over hers.

It was everything she had wished, everything her dream had promised...sinfully sweet and deliciously devouring; steamy, wet and wonderful. Her breasts grew heavy and her limbs weighted as his tongue stroked inside her, limber and strong, sliding against the slippery surfaces of her mouth, exploring the ripples in her arched palate and delving into the silky recesses beneath her tongue. He kissed and withdrew, kissed and withdrew, biting and sucking at her lips with each lingering withdrawal and slanting his head to make each invasion different...deeper, slower, longer...more flagrantly erotic...

She revelled in the straining tension of Matthew's body, time ceasing to matter as she felt his hands begin to move up her body, massaging it through the thin silk. When he came to her breasts, and found her nipples barricaded behind a wall of impenetrable lace, he uttered a whispered curse and kissed her with a punishing force that she returned in glorious measure, sinking her teeth into his lower lip and reaching down to draw teasing fingers across the taut bulge at the front of his trousers.

A rattle on the door-handle was all the warning they received as a freckle-faced young nurse suddenly invaded their illusion of privacy. They wrenched apart, far too late for any polite pretence as to what they'd been doing.

'Er...I just came in to get an extra pillow for a patient,' the nurse stammered, her eyes rounding at the sight of their flushed faces and rumpled clothes. Matthew recovered first, reaching up to pull one off the shelf just above them.

'Here, have this one.' His reddened mouth curved sardonically. 'We certainly weren't going to need it.'

He made it sound as if they had been about to make love standing up! Although goodness knows how far things would have gone if they hadn't been interrupted, Rachel was forced to concede. With a muffled sound of horror she noticed the photographs which Matthew had knocked off the shelf face-up under her feet, and bent to snatch them up, shielding them with her bulky bag.

'Thanks.' The nurse hugged the pillow to her breast as she backed towards the door, summoning the courage to venture, 'Umm...you're really not supposed to be doing—uh—what you're doing in here, you know...'

'Honey,' growled Matthew, '*we're* not supposed to be doing it *any*where!'

'She probably thinks we're a pair of guilty adulterers,' Rachel complained as they beat a hasty retreat. This time it didn't matter if she took the lift. She had already been thoroughly rumbled.

'Or a brother and sister,' he said, replacing his glasses as they stepped into the empty lift.

She looked at him in disgust, trying not to remember that only minutes ago she had been wax in his arms. 'Trust you to think of something perverted!'

He straightened his tie. 'I'm sure you could match me in perversity. We do seem to be making a habit of being caught *in flagrante delicto*.' He looked at her with a smile of grim satisfaction. 'And this latest incident certainly alters the stakes between us, doesn't it?'

'What do you mean?'

'Well, the blackmail game seems a little unproductive. I think I'm ready to graduate to something more…stimulating.'

'Like what?' asked Rachel, already guessing from his dangerous expression that she was going to hate his answer.

'Like kidnapping!'

CHAPTER SIX

RACHEL'S fingers hovered over the electronic box set flush into the white plaster wall, itching to try out the keypad. Birthdate? Wedding day?

'Forget it. It's tamper-proof.'

She whirled around as Matthew came up the internal staircase from his triple garage, carrying the by now crumpled photographs he had removed from her bag. She'd thought she had escaped him when she had broken away and made a dash for her car in the hospital car park, cramming her key into the nearside passenger door. But Matthew had foiled her by making an eye-opening leap across the sloping bonnet, sledding across the polished paintwork on his backside to land lightly on the other side and whip himself into the driver's seat in the time it took her to get inside.

'I always wanted to do that!' he had crowed smugly, plucking her keys from her frozen hand.

'You can't do this!' she spluttered, as he drove out of the car park with a cheerful wave of recognition to the amused security guard.

'I just did,' he pointed out, flicking on an indicator as he followed the sign for the motorway.

'But what about your Porsche—'

He shrugged. 'I'll have someone pick it up for me. Right now we have more important things to worry about...'

'Like my having you arrested for abduction?'

'Go ahead. Bring on the cops with their sirens and flashing lights,' he drawled sarcastically. 'Let's get as many people as possible involved in this sordid affair!'

She scowled. 'Where are you taking me?'

'Somewhere we won't be interrupted...'

The place to which he had brought her was certainly secluded. It lay in the rural belt south of the city, surrounded by the flat green fields and timber-railed fences of famous racing studs and training stables. The large white aggressively modern house was well tucked back from the road, on tree-studded land enclosed by a high stone wall and guarded by a state of-the-art remote video and alarm system.

'Not only does disarming it require a double code, but also a fingerprint ID,' Matthew informed her now, as she stood in the bare, white-walled foyer, the intensely coloured light cascading down from the domed leaded-glass skylight high overhead turning her hair into a vibrant cap of jewel-green as she tilted her head to warily monitor his approach. He held up a splayed hand, palm towards her. 'So, unless you're wearing the approved loops and whorls, all hell will break loose if you open a door anywhere in the house.'

She looked at all the closed doors she could see down the wide, straight hallway which passed beneath the graceful white arch of a double staircase leading to the upper floor.

'Then hadn't you better turn it off?' Even speaking softly, her voice echoed clearly in the empty space between the polished hardwood floors and the curving grained timber ceilings.

'I've turned off the sub-network that controls the internal doors and sound and motion sensors; I think I might leave the rest of the bells and whistles in place until you feel a trifle more...secure with my hospitality.'

She tossed her head, drawing herself up to her full height. 'May I at least have my car keys back?'

She fully expected him to refuse. Instead he took them out of his pocket and tossed them over.

'The garage doors are also operated on a code system,' he revealed as she snatched them out of the air. 'Are you thirsty? You look hot.' He turned on his heel and walked into the cool depths of the hallway, shedding his jacket and stripping off his tie. 'Coming?'

Curiosity drove her to follow without further protest. Underfoot the smooth wood changed to plush oriental carpet runners, rich with glowing colours woven into complex geometric patterns. Through half-open doors Rachel glimpsed large white-walled rooms, with more jewelled carpets decorating the wooden floors and only a very occasional piece of furniture. There seemed to be plenty of furniture on the walls, however, and she guessed that the art, rather than an obsession with personal safety, was the reason for the excessive security system.

The huge room into which Matthew turned looked out over a deep blue swimming pool fed by a waterfall and surrounded by pale flagstones and boulders of white rock.

Apart from a floor-to-ceiling bookcase running the length of the back wall, the only furniture was a sinuously curved waist-high cabinet topped with a waxed slab of recycled native timber growing out of another wall, and the long, serpentine ripple of an armless couch facing the glass doors, edged in lead-lights, that opened onto the pool.

He threw his jacket and tie across the top of the cabinet and laid the envelope down on top of them. From a refrigerator concealed in the bottom half of the cabinet Matthew took a bottle of mineral water and one of lager, silently offering her a choice. He poured her requested water into a large goblet of hand-blown glass, pushing it towards her across the intricately veined slab of wood, and did the same with a beer for himself.

'Isn't it a bit early in the day for that?' she attacked. 'If you're going to drink yourself into a stupor again I'd like to leave. In my experience you make an unpleasant drunk.'

He took a long draught of the icy liquid, watching her over the rim. 'Really? That's not what the pictures say.'

Her fingers clenched on her glass. 'You think I *enjoyed* what I had to do that night?' she said icily.

'*Had* to do?' he said, his narrow face hawkishly intent. 'Did someone somehow *force* you to lure me into a compromising position?'

Her glass clashed with the wood as she set it down, glaring belligerently across the bar. 'Of course not! And I didn't *lure* you—'

'But you *did* push me into that pool; there was never any oh-so-convenient *cat*, was there?' He smiled grimly as her face reflected her guilt. 'And I seem to remember *you* were the one who suggested the guest house...'

'Merrilyn was incapable of doing anything but panic; you were bombed out of your mind and threatening to create havoc—*somebody* had to decide what to do.'

'So it really was all your own idea,' he concluded bitterly. 'You still haven't told me *why*—was it some twisted form of revenge for not getting the contracts you wanted? For money? Or just for the sake of some sick head-game?'

He was making no sense. 'You're the one playing the games,' she flung at him. 'You tell *me*!'

He pushed away his unfinished beer and placed his hands flat on the bar. 'You're saying I get to make the first move?' he asked savagely. 'OK. How much?'

'How much what?'

'For the photographs—all prints and negatives. How much?'

She felt a sharp wrench in her chest. Foolishly she had somehow thought that he would relent, that he wouldn't let it go this far...

'You mean...how much money?' Her head whirled. He was asking *her* how much blackmail she was willing to pay?

'What do you think they're worth? Ten thousand?'

'Ten thousand dollars!' she echoed with an incredulous shrill.

'You think it should be more?' he asked sardonically 'How much? Twenty? Fifty grand? A hundred?'

'Don't be ridiculous!' she cried. He might as well ask for the moon. 'You're a *millionaire*, for God's sake. You don't need the money—'

'But you do? Why? To prop up that ailing business of yours?'

His scathing tone made her see red. 'It's not ailing. It's just a matter of smoothing out the cash flows.'

'And the way to do this is by indulging in a spot of blackmail? Hardly a good advertisement for your professional integrity.'

'I don't know what you're talking about—my integrity has never been in question!' she defended herself hotly. 'They're *your* photos. *You're* the blackmailer!'

'The hell I am!' He stared at her, feigning a thunderstruck innocence that made her blood boil.

She fished in her bag for her wallet and held up the green-inked note, now folded and angrily refolded many times. 'Then what's this? And don't tell me that you didn't write it, because—' she took another piece of paper from her wallet and held them side by side '—I compared it to this—the handwriting is identical.'

He looked at the formal apology he had sent with his

flowers, briefly diverted. 'You kept this? Did you press one of my flowers, too?'

She flushed. 'Don't flatter yourself.' She withered him with a lie. 'The roses went straight into the bin!'

He reached for the other note and she retracted it sharply. 'Oh, no, you don't—this is evidence. You mailed me those photographs and threatened to release them to the tabloids. You accused me of being a prostitute! And you have the nerve to accuse *me* of being somehow to blame!'

Dark blood began edging along the top of his cheekbones as he began to register the extent his error. 'But you sent them to me first—'

'I never saw them before in my life,' she blazed in righteous indignation. 'Not until you sent them to me with your sleazy note attached. And that envelope I gave your mother at the hospital *she* had just dropped. All I did was pick it up off the floor for her. If you think you can force us to withdraw Westons' bid for the KR contract without you having appeared to have interfered, you can think again! I have no idea where the photos came from, but if you have any more of them—'

'I don't, and I have no idea where they came from, either.'

'You can forget about trying—' She broke off her harangue. 'What did you say?'

He succinctly described the arrival of the envelope, addressed to his father at KR Industries, into his hands. 'There was no message, but I naturally assumed they were from you,' he said, rubbing his lean cheek, as if anticipating another well-deserved slap. 'I thought it was some kind of shakedown—'

'You *naturally* assumed?' Rachel was even more outraged. Her bosom heaved. 'Why was *I* the natural culprit?

What made you even *think* I was capable of such a despicable thing?'

'I don't know…maybe it was my subconscious.'

'Your subconscious told you I was a blackmailing bitch?' Her outraged voice bounced off the pitched ceiling.

Instead of flinching, he looked her straight in the eye and said with devastating honesty, 'No, my subconscious was telling me that you were a gorgeous, earthy, incredibly sexy woman to whom I was dangerously attracted. I say "dangerously" because all my logical thought-processes went completely haywire whenever you were in the vicinity. In trying to hide it I guess I might have overcompensated. You may have noticed that I hardly managed to address a single coherent sentence to you whenever we were in a room together…'

Rachel felt as if she had been hit on the head, dazed by this insight—so totally at odds with her own interpretation of his dismissive behaviour.

'If couldn't trust my own instincts or judgement where you were concerned,' he said, seeming satisfied by her stunned silence. 'How could I trust you? I felt furious, betrayed…but I was excited, too. I *wanted* it to be you, because it would licence me to act on my passions in the cause of natural justice…'

'I—you…I don't know what you expect me to say…' she stammered, intensely flustered.

'Should I send you some more roses?' he murmured, removing his spectacles to bare his black-eyed gaze.

'*No!*' She couldn't help thinking of what had happened the last time he had taken off his glasses. 'No…'

'You were equally quick to think badly of me, so in a sense we're even,' he slyly pointed out.

'I had the better reason,' she flashed. 'And Neville said—'

'Ah, *Neville*.' He cut her off, his expression suddenly shuttered. 'I don't doubt my dear cousin cast me in a rather unflattering light…'

The full implications of what he had said were only now beginning to sink in. Rachel stared sightlessly at the notes in her hand. 'I—why are you so willing to trust me now?'

Annoyed by the husky tenor of her voice, she looked up at him, hardening her expression. He needn't think that just because he had confessed to being *dangerously attracted*, she would overlook everything that he had said and done. 'And why should *I* believe what *you* tell me?'

'Perhaps because we both know each other a little better now,' he said, moving around the bar. 'Truce?'

She flushed. 'If you think that a few kisses constitutes knowing someone better—'

He studied her blush. 'Actually, I was talking about our mutual investigations. The man I have watching you says that you have a reputation in your neighbourhood for being a soft touch for those in trouble, but you're scrupulous about old-fashioned principles like honesty and fair dealing.'

'You've had me under *surveillance*?' she bristled. She had been so busy keeping tabs on *him* that it had never occurred to her to look over her shoulder.

'It seemed like a good idea at the time.' He shrugged. 'Of course, if I'd known that you were going to start shadowing *me*, perhaps I could have saved myself the expense.'

'You *knew* I was following you?' She remembered how naively pleased she had been with herself the previous night.

'Well, not until my detective came in with his report while I was visiting Dad—and told me that you had just accosted my mother on the ward,' he admitted.

At least it was some consolation that he hadn't spotted

her himself! She knew it would be hypocritical to voice her fierce objection to the invasion of her privacy.

'I hope he's costing you an arm and a leg,' she contented herself with snapping.

'I get a discount—he's with the firm that does the security work for Ayr Holdings. The same one that beat yours out of those contracts,' he said, adding insult to injury.

'I suppose he's the one you'll get to pick up your Porsche—'

'No, actually I told him his input would no longer be necessary, that I'd handle it myself from here on...'

Rachel folded her arms over her chest. 'Did you show him the photographs?'

Matthew's eyes glowed with quiet understanding. 'I haven't shown anyone. I never even mentioned the word "blackmail". As far as he was concerned it was simply a straightforward case of me wanting to find out more about you.'

She stiffened. 'Are you having the bill charged to Ayr Holdings or to a private account?' she asked.

'Privately,' he admitted.

'I see. So he knows it's something you don't want going through the books, then. He probably thinks that you're vetting me as a potential mistress,' she said sourly.

'Lover.'

The soft word caressed her senses like a fur glove. 'What?'

'Just being precise. You could only be my mistress if I was already married. Since I'm not, that would make you my prospective lover rather than my kept woman.' As she scrabbled for a sufficiently devastating answer he added: 'But why set your sights so low? Maybe he thought I was checking out your suitability as a potential wife...'

Her heart gave a sickening thump. She tossed her head.

'What makes you think that marriage to you would be such an elevation? Anyway, men who're contemplating a new marriage generally don't continue to wear their old wedding rings...'

He twisted the thick gold band on his finger. 'Is that a piece of detective school lore?' He slid the heavy ring off his finger and rolled it in his palm. 'I must say it's been very useful for keeping the society she-wolves at bay. You've no idea the offers I was inundated with after Leigh died...'

She could imagine, and for that reason she was sour. 'The rich never have to be lonely for long.'

He slipped the ring into his trouser pocket. 'I never bought into the illusion that sex is an adequate substitute for love, and a love that has to be bought isn't worth the investment. What about you?'

'What about me?' She looked at him wide-eyed, startled by the discovery that beneath the sophisticated shell Matthew Riordan was a romantic.

'After David Weston died did you take up any male offers of comfort?'

'Why are you asking? I'm sure by now you have a full list of my ex-lovers,' she said sniffily.

'I was interested in your present, not past, and at present there doesn't seem to be any man in your life. Unless you and your partner have a secret thing going...'

'Frank?' Her jolt of incredulous laughter brought a subtle curve of satisfaction to his mouth.

He leaned on elbow on the bar. 'You don't find him attractive?'

'He's handsome enough, I suppose, but we've never particularly hit it off.' She shrugged. 'He's hardly irresistible.'

'Is that what you're looking for? A man whom you find yourself totally unable to resist? That's not very PC of you.'

'Since when has political correctness had anything to do with it? And I'm not *looking* at all. I'm quite content with my life as it is!' she lied, with a fierceness that rang slightly hollow.

'So…what did Weston say when you told him I was blackmailing you?'

'What makes you think I'd automatically go running to Frank? I can handle my own problems.'

He raised his eyebrows. 'You haven't told him? I would have thought you'd value his professional opinion.'

'I haven't told anyone. If Frank knew about those photos there'd be nothing professional about his attitude.' She shuddered. 'He'd go totally ape!'

He straightened, frowning, his shoulders tensing under the tailored blue cotton. 'You mean you're afraid he might get violent. Has he hurt you before?'

'No, of course not! I didn't mean physically. But he'd probably demand I disassociate myself from Westons, and I wouldn't blame him!'

'*I* would. You were his brother's fiancé; surely he'd stand by you?'

'I told you, we're not that close. He'd consider that I'd brought it on myself by being careless. And I was. Someone else followed us to that room and took those photos, and I didn't even notice.'

'Neither did I.'

'Matthew, you weren't in any condition to notice *any*-thing, or do anything about it if you *had*.'

Seeing that she was determined to punish herself with the full blame, he was equally determined that she should not.

'I beg to differ. For example, I certainly noticed a great deal about *you*…and if I hadn't been in a condition to do something about it you wouldn't have had to tie me to the bed.'

He had the pleasure of seeing her wrestle with the urge to explode, her self-control only winning by the narrowest of margins as she clipped, 'Dammit, I should have been more careful.'

It was time someone forced her to acknowledge that she sometimes needed help. 'How?'

'I don't know.' She raked her hand through her hair, drawing his attention to the flawless sheen of sun-kissed skin at her temples and the thickness of the lashes that fringed her frowning hazel eyes. The lips he had so recently kissed were compressed into a prim line which he knew was a lie. The lady's disdain was only skin-deep; under that armour of tough self-sufficiency was a passion as reckless as it was strong.

'Don't beat yourself up over it. No one could have planned for things to turn out exactly the way they did that night,' he told her. 'There were too many variables involved, so it had to be a purely spur-of-the-moment thing. Someone saw an opportunity and grabbed it. You were only involved because you were in the wrong place at the wrong time. There's been no demand for money, so this isn't a straightforward case of financial extortion—this is a vindictive act, a smear aimed at the Riordans—specifically *me*.'

So now he was relegating her from starring role in a drama to bit-player in a farce?

'Without a note we can't know that for sure,' she said hotly. 'They might be intended to destroy my character in your father's eyes—make me seem like a danger to his family and thus wreck any chance of anyone associated with me ever getting any business from KR.'

'And who would benefit most from that?'

'Directly? Well, the other security companies who are making competitive bids, I suppose.'

'And are they really likely to use that kind of dirty trick against one of their own, at considerable risk to their own reputations?' he asked. 'A thing like that could boomerang and be as much a threat to themselves as to you.'

Put like that it sounded highly unlikely. Rachel had been so certain of Matthew's guilt that she hadn't bothered to ponder any solid alternatives.

'Well, how many enemies do *you* have?' she challenged.

He shrugged. 'Since Dad has started telling people I'm thinking of standing for local body elections all sorts of cranks have come out of the woodwork. In my opinion anyone who isn't a friend is potentially an enemy.'

She was appalled by such cynicism. 'Why leave out your friends?' she said cattily.

He laughed, and picked up the envelope and his beer. 'Because they're such a rare and precious breed. The only way to have a friend is to be one. Prosperity has plenty of glittering acquaintances—real friendship sticks around for trouble...like now...'

She faced him, arms akimbo. 'I'm not your friend. I'm only here because you didn't give me any choice.'

'A friend in need is a friend indeed—we're both in this together, Rachel, whether you like it or not. Come on, we have some homework to do...'

To Rachel's embarrassment, ''homework'' consisted of comparing memories with Matthew, who lay on his stomach on the bare floor in a patch of sunlight minutely examining the latest photographs, which he proclaimed as identical to the first three.

'So, we could conclude that there probably are no more—the photographer just managed to get these few shots, not a whole roll of film—otherwise why wouldn't he have sent pictures progressively more explicit and therefore threatening—'

'Because it didn't *get* any more explicit!' Rachel proclaimed, from her lofty perch on the couch.

He rolled on his side and propped his head on his hand. 'Didn't it?'

She looked suspiciously down into his narrow handsome face. 'Don't you *know*?'

'I told you.' He grinned. 'My recollection gets a bit hazy after the bondage bit... My doctor said you told him I was delirious.'

She took a gulp of her water. 'There was no bondage! I *temporarily restrained* you—*gently*—when you tried to pull down my dress—'

'After you had undressed me...'

'Your clothes were wet and you wouldn't take them off for yourself. Your doctor said I did the right thing.'

'So we didn't make love?' he asked wistfully.

All this time he had thought they might have been *lovers*?

'No! What kind of woman do you think I am? No, don't answer that,' she said hastily as he opened his mouth. 'Believe me, Matthew—nothing *happened*.'

'But we wanted it to... I seem to remember—'

'That you were confused—you had a fever,' she reminded him.

'Mmm, you look as if you were pretty hot yourself,' he murmured, returning to his study.

Rachel felt that way now. 'Matthew—'

'Matt.'

She gritted her teeth. 'Is it necessary to use a magnifying glass?'

'How closely did you look at the photos I sent you?'

'I didn't drool over every minute detail with a magnifying glass, if that's what you mean!'

'Then you should have…come down and look at this.'

'I've seen all I need to see—'

'I doubt it. Come on, Rachel, it's a bit too late for false modesty.' He stretched over and laced his fingers around her ankle, giving it a little tug. 'This is important.'

'Oh, all right.' She shook off his hand and reluctantly knelt down beside his prone figure, taking the magnifying glass he handed her.

'Look, there…'

Her face went fiery red as she saw his finger tracing the curve of her bare hip where it joined her torso 'You—'

'Rachel…' His hand clamped around hers on the handle of the glass, forcing it to remain poised over the glossy still. 'Get over it! Try and forget for a moment that this is you and me. This photograph has been altered, so seamlessly it couldn't have been done in a darkroom—it has to have been done on a computer.

'I'm only guessing, but I doubt your bottom is really as slim as it appears to be here—and see the strange angle of your hips in relation to the position of your thighs? Look at the length from hip to knee—those legs don't belong to a woman of your height—and where's the muscle definition of a woman who works out as much as you do in the gym? Then there's the evenness of the skin toning below your waist—is that natural, given the lighting in the room? I bet if you scanned this and looked at it pixel by pixel you'd be able to see the joins…'

'My God—this isn't me!' Rachel realised gratefully, collapsing on her stomach beside him, leaning on her elbows, her hair brushing his cheek as she jostled him for a better look. 'This is all a fake!'

'Well, not *all*…the top half is pretty unmistakably you,'

he pointed out. 'And that's definitely me there underneath you…'

She was obeying his advice and concentrating fiercely on the details. 'I didn't *think* my dress had been dragged down that far, but I thought it must have slipped south in the struggle. I remember having to do a lot of wriggling and twisting to get it back up again…'

'So do I,' he sighed reminiscently, earning himself a sharp nudge in the shoulder.

'Why didn't it occur to me that this had to be a fake?' she castigated herself.

'Probably because, like me, you were initially too furious to think rationally, and also because the other two photographs *are* perfectly genuine—if misleading,' he said. 'Whoever did this is clever, and has all the right ingredients: a good digital scanner, some sophisticated computer software, a pile of porn, a lot of patience and a gutful of resentment.'

'And the whip,' she discovered, shifting the thick optic lens, 'that's been scanned in, too. Did you notice, Matt? It's supposedly lying on the sheet, but it's not making any dent in the folds…'

'Well, on reflection, it did seem unlikely that a woman as forceful as yourself would need a whip to keep a man in line,' he said. 'Especially when you already have a tongue far more stinging than any lash.'

She glanced sideways to find his expression teasing. Their eyes met, and for the first time she found herself tempted to laugh over her ghastly predicament.

'I gather you've changed your mind about my being a professional dominatrix?' She referred sweetly to his coruscating note.

His eyelids flickered, and although he steadily held her gaze, his colour rose. 'I doubt you'd want, or expect, abject submission from a man in your bed. I think you're far more likely to demand an equal exchange of passion...'

He imagined she'd be demanding in bed! He probably thought of her as an experienced older woman, Rachel told herself, alarmed at how arousing she found the notion. She'd never been with a younger man—David had been eleven years her senior. She latched onto the memory in a desperate attempt to anchor herself to sober reality.

She cleared her throat and sat up. 'What are we going to do about these?' She indicated the photos.

'I'm glad to hear you say "we",' he said, stacking them up and helping her to her feet with inbred politeness. 'I take it you're no more keen than I am to have the police involved?'

She shuddered, and shook her head. 'I may as well just tell Frank! The fewer people who know, the less chance of a leak.'

'Then the first thing we need to do is to neutralise the threat those pictures represent by destroying their capacity to create a scandal. That'll give us the freedom to organise a more thorough investigation.'

Rachel tensed suspiciously at the latter statement. 'But no outsiders—and as far as I'm concerned that includes your security people.'

She continued to hammer the point as she followed him out of the room and across the hallway into a stunning white kitchen, where Matthew calmly busied himself making her a snack, after prying out of her that her lunch on stake-out had been a meagre sandwich and an apple.

'Not nearly enough for someone who burns as much energy as you,' he told her, opening the gigantic doubledoored refrigerator.

Was that an oblique reference to her size? No—if

Matthew wanted to comment on her curves he would do it frankly.

'I haven't really been very hungry the last few days— I'm still recovering from flu,' she protested half-heartedly, her mouth watering as she watched him skilfully chop chicken, celery and a hard-boiled egg and deftly fold them into sour cream sprinkled with capers, fresh parsley and chives.

'Which I take it is also my fault?' he said, spooning the mixture into a cup of a lettuce and sliding the plate across the tiled breakfast bar where she sat. 'But I can solemnly promise you, Rachel, that's the only kind of infection you risk catching from me in bed.' He smiled at her expression. 'Surely by now you've guessed that's how I hope we're going to end up? By being upfront now we can enjoy the spontaneity later...'

While she was still gaping at his staggering presumption he forked up a morsel of salad and popped it between her parted lips. As her mouth closed and she automatically began to chew he handed her the implement and distracted her from the fact she was eating, with a string of amusing stories about his brash father's cunning machinations to free Matthew from the social stigma of being a *nouveau riche* rubbish-man's son.

Without realising it, Rachel allowed him to draw forth wry recollections of her far less privileged home background, and the impact her unplanned arrival had had on a mother and father who had already discovered the first time around that they were not natural parents. Their love had been strictly rationed according to behaviour; their expectations as low as Kevin Riordan's had been high.

A fragrant cup of spiced tea eventually replaced her empty plate, and Rachel realised they had strayed far from the purpose of her enforced visit. She hurriedly returned to their discussion of tactics, and when he objected to her insistence on pursuing her own separate avenues of investigation, her heated accusations prompted him to frankly spell out exactly why Weston Security had lost its bids.

'It was *not* because of my personal reaction to you.' He refuted her bitter allegation with passionate conviction. 'I wouldn't survive very long at the head of a financial empire if I let my emotions, however intense, dictate my business decisions. Nor was it from any prejudice against women— some of my brightest executives are female.'

He listed a string of salient factors that forced Rachel to acknowledge that perhaps *she* had been the one guilty of prejudice, her hindsight coloured by the disparaging remarks that Neville had dripped in her ear.

She found herself agreeing that she would take no steps without full consultation, but made no promises that she would accept any resulting advice.

'Let's remember that *I'm* the professional in this field; you're just a—'

'Gifted amateur?'

'*Bumbling* amateur,' she corrected.

'Oh, I get it. I'm Watson to your Holmes.'

She frowned. 'This isn't a game.'

'No, but that doesn't mean we can't enjoy it.'

She felt a little tingle in her bones, not of foreboding but of illicit excitement. 'You said something before about neutralising any scandal...'

She turned to watch him carry the dishes to the dishwasher and caught sight of the kitchen clock high on the wall. She checked it disbelievingly against her watch, appalled to see that the whole afternoon had slipped effortlessly away. She leapt to her feet, determined to assert herself, only to find her erstwhile kidnapper effusively helpful.

Quite how Matthew had persuaded her to allow him to drive her home in her own car she couldn't afterwards remember, but she knew it was a mistake as soon as he introduced himself to Robyn on the doorstep and insinuated himself inside to accept an offer of a cup of tea and endure a sisterly interrogation.

Looking perfectly at ease in the modest drawing room, he sipped his tea and listened to Robyn chatter about her last day at work, and proved so charming that when Rachel reminded him for the fourth time about the taxi he had supposedly come inside to call it was Robyn who leapt up and rushed away to do it.

'I suppose using your cellphone was out of the question,' Rachel said, knowing that he probably never went anywhere without a lifeline to the financial markets.

'I think the battery's flat,' he lied blatantly, as the front door slammed open and shut again, and feet pounded up the hall just ahead of an excited voice.

'Hey, guess what—my class threw a farewell party for me at school today!' Bethany skidded to a stop in the door, her hazel eyes and pink mouth rounding in recognition at the sight of the man rising politely to his feet. 'Wow, it's the babe!'

'I beg your pardon?' Matthew held out his hand, looking amused. 'I'm Matt Riordan.'

Bethany laughed as she shook it. 'You're the man from the photo—the one who was kissing Rachel's hand at that party.'

Only Rachel noticed the tip of his ears go pink. 'You *saw* those photos?'

'I opened them at the breakfast table,' Rachel said cruelly.

'I only looked at one—Rachel hid all the others. Were they horribly obscene or something?' asked Bethany.

'Utterly,' he grinned, slanting Rachel a sly look.

Bethany was sharp-eyed. She tilted up her chin. 'Are you

and Rachel going out on a date?' There was mingled curiosity and disappointment in her voice.

He shook his head. 'I know this is your last night here,
and you probably want to spend it together. Actually, I'm
here to ask *you* for one.'

'Me?'

'I know Rachel is planning to see you and your mother
off to Bangkok tomorrow evening, and I thought that you
might allow me to take all three of you out to lunch and
then run you over to the airport in my father's limousine.'

'Matt—'

'You mean a proper black limo with a chauffeur—a
stretch?' The young girl cut eagerly across Rachel's faint
protest.

'With a TV, video and computer in the back,' Matthew
confirmed. 'You can e-mail your friends goodbye on the
way to the airport.'

Bethany's eyes gleamed. 'We've got *hu-mung-ous*
amounts of luggage!' she warned. 'We're taking *everything*.'

'Then I guess we'll make that two limos—one for us and
one for your luggage.'

Bethany giggled and flushed shyly. 'Are you serious?'
He nodded, and she instantly beamed again. 'That would
be fabulous, wouldn't it, Rachel? Some of the gang are
coming to see me off—imagine their faces when I swan up
in a *limo*! Does Mum know? Let me tell her!'

She bounced out of the room, only to pop her head back
around the door and say mischievously, 'I guess this means
you've changed your mind about him being a slimy, scum-
sucking slug, huh, Rachel?'

He stroked his lean jaw, studying her discomfiture. 'A
slug?'

'It seemed apposite at the time,' said Rachel stoutly. 'About tomorrow—I don't think—'

'Come off it, Rachel, you know you aren't going to disappoint her. This way you all get to have a good time instead of moping around here prolonging your goodbyes. And Robyn won't have to worry about you being left on your own.' He glanced towards the door. 'Bethany's a very pretty girl.'

Rachel just stopped herself from saying thank you. 'Yes, yes, she is.'

'She's the spitting image of you—same eyes, same shape of face, same challenging heft of the chin when she takes on a dare... She's probably going to be as tall as you are, too,' he said in idle speculation.

'Yes...'

'In fact she looks far more like you than she does Robyn—' He stopped as he saw her face, and she hurriedly bent to put the empty teacups back onto the wooden tray.

'Rachel?'

She didn't answer him, and when she looked again he was standing by the window, looking at the little clutch of photographs on the side table, seeing the progression of Rachel from freckle-faced child stiffly posed between dour-faced parents to the laughing woman at David's side. And looking at the photos of Robyn, Bethany and Simon.

'Rachel?' He looked across at her, the knowledge dawning in his brown eyes, his expression deeply shaken. 'Bethany is *your* child, isn't she, not Robyn's?'

She nodded jerkily and he crossed the room, his voice low as he checked towards the door. 'Does she know?'

'Of course she does,' said Rachel fiercely. 'Robyn and Simon have always been honest with her about her adoption. She knows they can't conceive a baby themselves and that I—I couldn't look after the one that *I'd* conceived...'

His eyes darkened with turbulent emotion. 'But, my God, you must have been only—'

'Fifteen,' she said, to save him the calculation. 'The same age that Bethany is now...'

A freckle-faced half-child, half-woman, as delicate and fresh as a half-unfurled bud, thought Matthew.

To Rachel's shock he didn't ask about Bethany's father, or the circumstances of her birth. Instead he touched a gentle finger to her pale lips in a gentle salute.

'Congratulations on your wonderful daughter...and on the courage and strength it must have taken you to bring her into the world...'

Her eyes stung as he replaced his finger with a gossamer-light touch of his lips and an admiring whisper.

'Until tomorrow, my brave lioness...'

CHAPTER SEVEN

'WHAT in the hell is going on?'

'Frank!' Rachel was startled to see her partner on her front doorstep, a folded newspaper clutched in his fist. After David died their social contact had dwindled sharply, and since she had been working full-time at WSS they rarely met outside the office. She knew Frank usually spent his Saturdays catching up with paperwork, on call for any problems with the weekend roster.

'Uh, come in,' she invited belatedly as he brushed past her. 'Robyn and Bethany have just gone out to say goodbye to Simon's mother—' she began, wondering if he had come to make his farewells.

Frank swung around just inside the door, his fair skin flushed with anger. 'Since when have you been seeing Matthew Riordan?' he interrupted harshly. 'I thought we were supposed to be on the same side? You let me run off my mouth about him—you even agreed that he was a stiff-necked bastard who had it in for us—and now I find out that you two are secretly an item! Do you know what a bloody fool this makes me look?'

He didn't wait for an answer, bulldozing on in a fury. 'I can't believe you let things go this far without telling me. Instead I had to read it in the morning paper along with everybody else!' he spat, thrusting the newspaper under her nose.

Rachel's heart plunged as she took it with shaking fingers. 'What're you talking about? I don't get the weekend papers—'

'I'm talking about that!' Frank's thick finger stabbed forcefully at the article folded uppermost—a few paragraphs under a small photograph of Matt wearing a faint social smile that made him look flatteringly enigmatic. 'It says a lot of crap about your engagement being the result of a "whirlwind romance"—it must have been one hell of a whirlwind since you only met couple of months ago and you always acted like you couldn't stand him. I thought Riordan was supposed to be getting married to some snotty society woman!'

Jolted by his angry crudity, Rachel blinked with eyes that refused to focus, her brain scrambling to sort out the black and white print.

'I—I don't know where they got this—' she faltered.

'I do. I rang the paper as soon as I saw it,' Frank rapped. 'That was a press release from Riordan's publicist. The whole *world* knows you're engaged to the man—didn't you think you owed me even a *hint*?'

His words hit Rachel between the eyes.

The whole world knows you're engaged... What scandal was there in a man playing sex games with his fiancé in the privacy of their own bedroom?

This was how Matt planned to 'neutralise' any blackmail threat? Without even *warning* her?

'But I—this isn't right...'

His blue eyes were pebble-hard. 'You're telling me it's not true?' he snapped. 'That you didn't leap at the chance to investigate him so you could spend more time with your *lover*?'

'I—'

'Where were you yesterday afternoon, anyway? I couldn't get you on your cellphone.'

She remembered the posters in the coronary ward, warning that portable phones could interfere with monitoring equipment. 'I'm sorry. I turned it off and forgot to switch it back on.'

He was quick to pounce on the hint of guilt. 'You were with *him*, weren't you?' And as her flush deepened he swore. 'So it *is* true!'

'I'm sorry, Frank.' She indicated the paper. 'But I didn't know he was going to do this—'

'So that makes it all right? Is there anything *else* you should have told me?'

She had said she wasn't frightened of him, but she hesitated to add further fuel to his blazing fury. She shook her head helplessly and that seemed to uncork the full force of his rage.

'You really think you can have it all, don't you, Rachel? You're living here in Dave's house, on the back of his business, and you're sneaking around with a guy who's threatening everything that Dave and I built up! You didn't utter a peep when I told you about Riordan taking over at KR. Maybe you already knew! I guess sleeping with the enemy means that your loyalty counts for nothing any more.'

Rachel was winded by his punches. 'This has nothing to do with David. And I haven't slept with Matthew—'

'Oh, been holding out for marriage, have you?' he sneered. 'And now you've had a taste of the high life with Mr Moneybags, I suppose you'd like to conveniently forget Dave ever existed. He always said you were hard-headed and practical—I call it having an eye out for the main chance. But just remember there's no profit in being dead! Ask yourself why, if he was such a crash-hot husband, the first Mrs Riordan topped herself!'

There was more, bitter, personal invective that left Rachel pale and shaken.

'I think you'll find that getting engaged to Riordan and

getting him to marry you are two entirely different things. He's just amusing himself with you. You haven't got the right connections. He may be loaded, but he comes from trash and he knows it. Men like him always marry up, not down!'

Robyn and Bethany arrived back just as he was delivering his parting shot, almost bumped off the garden path by his headlong rush.

'What's his problem?' Robyn watched him roar off in his car and frowned at Rachel's pale cheeks. 'What's he been saying?'

Rachel managed to summon a thin smile. 'Nothing he hasn't been thinking for a long time, I suppose. Maybe it was just temper talking,' she said generously, trying to put the ugly accusations into perspective. 'I always knew he didn't think I was good enough for David; I just didn't expect him to throw it up at me again after all this time. I thought we'd at least learned to respect each other.'

'I never did like Frank very much,' said Robyn flatly. 'I don't think he's capable of trusting anyone—he never even trusted David to decide what was best for himself, did he? It never occurred to him that his precious brother was *lucky* to find a woman who loved him as much as you did! What put him in such a temper, anyway?'

'Uh...' Rachel hid the crumpled newspaper behind her back, surreptitiously trying to stuff it down the back of the telephone table.

Fortunately Bethany came up beside her mother and distracted her beautifully by asking Rachel when she was planning to get ready for their promised lunch.

'But I am ready,' protested Rachel, looking down at her white overshirt, blue boat-necked top and cropped narrow trousers.

Robyn and Bethany looked at each other and rolled their eyes. 'Oh, no, you're not!' they chorused.

Rachel's strenuous protests fell on deaf ears as they bore her off to plunder the contents of her wardrobe.

'Hey, I remember this!' said Robyn, discovering the purple linen halterneck dress with its gauzy see-through jacket pushed to the back of the closet. 'David bought this for you, didn't he?'

'No one wears halternecks any more,' objected Rachel, eyeing the deep neckline.

'Are you kidding? The retro look is hot. I saw a designer dress like this in last month's *Vogue*,' said Bethany, sealing her fate.

'I probably won't get into it—it always was rather snug...'

If anything she seemed to have lost weight since she had last worn it.

'This is ridiculous. I'm way overdressed,' she grumbled, turning away from the sight of the three of them in the mirror, realising with a pang that it might be a very long time before she had her sister and daughter to chivvy her over feminine fripperies.

'Then we'll all look ridiculous together—we're dressed up too,' pointed out Robyn. 'But I bet Matthew won't think so...' she added smugly.

By the time he arrived Bethany was in a fever of expectation, dashing out to the gate to greet him, coltishly graceful in her multi-coloured slip-dress and white lace cardigan.

'I thought you said there'd be two of them!' she pouted as the chauffeur began to marshal their bags.

'Kale assures me that this thing has a boot like the hold of a 747,' grinned Matt, following her up the path to help with the luggage.

'Ladies...' His eyes politely admired Robyn's classic

mint-green ensemble, but lingered on the purple dress with a smouldering pleasure that he made no effort to disguise. This morning his spectacles were narrow rectangles rimmed in silver. He saw her looking at them and adjusted them unnecessarily on his aquiline nose.

'They're not new—I have a whole wardrobe of them,' he said, with a tinge of defensiveness that caused Rachel to hide a smile.

'Vanity, thy name is man,' she said, amused by the chink in his armour. 'Can't you wear contacts?'

He looked even more self-conscious. 'Lenses aren't as convenient when you're not a full-time wearer, and my short-sightedness is only marginal. I simply prefer glasses.'

'Because they make you appear like a mild-mannered intellectual rather than the ruthless competitor you really are?' Something in his expression prompted a leap of intuition. 'Are they part of that cool image you like to project? Do you use them to help fend off some of those society she-wolves, on the principal that girls don't make passes at guys who wear glasses…?'

'Well, the superficial types do tend not to look beyond the face furniture.' His bland reply neither confirmed nor denied the allegation.

'Then they must be dim-witted as well as superficial, because—' She hurriedly cut herself off, but too late for the spark of laughter that lit his eyes.

'What? You find them sexy?' He lowered them on his nose to peer at her over the top of them. 'Do we share a secret fantasy about you seducing a certain seemingly mild-mannered intellectual? Stripping off his spectacles along with his—*oof!*' He doubled over the suitcase that Rachel thrust into his stomach.

'Here, how about flexing a muscle *other* than your tongue!'

'Oh, believe me, I am,' he murmured wickedly, laughing as she flounced away in a flutter of purple.

He managed the heavy suitcase with surprising ease, and Rachel found herself surreptitiously watching the flex of his body as he hefted it over the raised lip of the boot. In cream trousers and a pale jacket over a white shirt with a yellow tie he managed to look both elegant and summery, and she was suddenly glad she had let herself be bullied into wearing something bold. She would need all the help she could get to hold her own against him for the next few hours.

In the bustle of loading there was no chance of taxing him about his press release, but, after making a final check of the empty spare bedrooms and locking up, she managed a brief exchange as they walked back to the limo.

'I need to talk to you,' she threatened under her breath.

He had the audacity to look innocent. 'About?'

'About a certain *engagement*,' she ground out.

'Can you think of any better way to take the heat off us?' he asked in an equally low tone.

The problem was that she couldn't. 'Promise you won't say anything to Robyn?' she hissed, balking as he tried to hand her in to the back of the car.

'Trust me,' he said, with a sweet smile that made her insides do a strange flip. 'I won't say anything to worry your sister.' He slid along the bench seat with her, settling to face Robyn and Bethany and draping his arm along the back of the seat behind her silky head.

Bethany made the most of their luxurious ride, and when they arrived at the restaurant Robyn smirked across at her sister.

'Aren't you glad you dressed up? I told you he'd be taking us somewhere posh!'

The restaurant was an elegant old house set in park-like

grounds, and in between the prearranged courses they strolled the gardens, feeding the goldfish in the numerous ponds and admiring the peacocks parading their pride on the jewel-green lawns. Once again, Matthew proved himself capable of disconcerting charm, gently teasing Bethany into feeling comfortable with the formal service and ensnaring Robyn's professional interest and personal sympathy with talk of his father's imminent by-pass surgery, managing to casually drop into the conversation the fact that Rachel had met both his parents. Robyn's attention was also kept busy monitoring the small courtesies Matthew constantly paid to Rachel.

'You know, you should wear clothes like that more often,' he told her, his warm brown eyes enjoying the visual feast she presented. 'You have such a superbly majestic figure it's a shame to swamp it in layers of fabric. And that particular shade is perfect for your colouring; it gives your skin a kind of lustrous glow...'

'David chose this dress for me,' she informed him with a hint of belligerence.

'Then he obviously had excellent taste—in both clothes and women,' he said quietly, with an exquisite diplomacy that made Robyn sigh gustily.

As they progressed through the leisurely meal Rachel was forced to admire his ability to appear to be frank and open while cleverly avoiding contentious issues and retaining firm control of the conversation. She remembered that he had cut his financial teeth in the maverick world of foreign exchange dealing, and now she saw the qualities that had enabled him to excel in those pressure-cooker conditions, to make lightning decisions involving millions of dollars based on calculated risks that sane men would reject as reckless. Since he had assumed the mantle at Ayr Holdings he had relinquished his maverick status to become the epitome of solid conservatism, but now she realised that under that respectable façade the volatile taker of extreme risks still existed, albeit constrained by maturity and experience.

Rachel ate the delicious food and drank the champagne, refusing to dwell on the implications of her sudden insight.

Later, en route to the airport, as she was beginning to tense at the thought of the coming ordeal, Matthew took her hand in his and pressed it against his taut thigh.

'I know Rachel hasn't told you much about us, but perhaps I'd better warn you…'

Rachel's arm jerked, but the strong masculine fingers were too determined to allow her to pull free.

'About what?' asked Robyn, her eyes darting expectantly between them.

'Just that you might be hearing some news from us soon.'

'What news?'

Matthew gave her a limpid smile. 'It would be premature to say. Your sister is a very independent and stubborn female.'

Robyn chuckled back, relaxing again in her seat. 'She is that. She's always been a fighter.'

Matthew's hand tested his jaw. 'I can certainly attest to that,' he said drily. 'I just thought you'd like to know she has someone else on her side.'

'Good—she needs someone. Since Mum and Dad retired to the Gold Coast there's no help from that quarter…not that they were ever much of a support—too busy living their own lives and protecting their precious respectability. And Frank is a dead loss. You should have seen the way he stormed out of our place this morning.'

'Frank Weston came to see you?' Matthew looked sharply at Rachel, taking a shrewd guess as to the reason for his visit, but it was Robyn who answered, telling him about the angry visit that had left Rachel so upset.

'I don't know what he was so furious about, but he had no right to pitch into Rachel about David. He always was a hard-nosed cynic, but you'd think he'd have got over his jealousy by now.'

'Of David?'

Rachel simmered at Matthew's swift curiosity. Did he think she was the type of woman to play one brother off against another?

Robyn burbled on. 'No—of *Rachel* and David—because they were so great together. It's all water under the bridge now, anyway. I told her that he might ease up if she appealed to his sense of justice—told him about all this other stuff she's spooked about at the moment—but of course she won't.'

'All what other stuff?'

'Robyn, no—'

But her sister was in full throttle now as she enlarged on the harassments that Rachel had endured over the past few months and her recently expressed theory that they were part of a deliberate campaign.

Sensing the pressure of his interest, Rachel uttered an inner sigh of relief as the international terminal came into view and Bethany bobbed up out of the sunroof and began shrieking and waving to her friends as they pulled up in the drop-off zone.

The tedium of the check-in was considerably relieved when Robyn and Bethany were drawn aside from the queue by a uniformed representative from the airline to be told that they had been upgraded to First Class, and given access cards to the hospitality lounge where they could relax in luxury before their flight.

Robyn was the first to twig. 'Matt, did you have anything to do with this?'

'We do a considerable amount of corporate business with this airline,' he admitted with a self-deprecating smile. 'What's the use of having influence if you can't use it on behalf of your friends?'

'First Class!' Robyn hugged her ticket blissfully. 'Now I'm *really* glad we didn't wear jeans and T-shirts!'

Robyn and Bethany were so elated that they were eager to go through to the departure lounge, and after they had browsed through the duty-free shops Matthew sensitively excused himself to give the three females sufficient time for their private farewells.

Rachel bore up well until they reached the departure gate and exchanged final hugs.

Robyn held her snugly close and whispered teasingly in her ear, 'He's a gentleman, Rach, definitely a keeper— don't let him slip through your fingers!'

Bethany exchanged last, tearful words with her excited school friends, and managed a wobbly smile with her hug.

'Be happy,' said Rachel simply, smoothing the blonde hair back from her daughter's clear forehead. 'And don't let your mother drink too much free champagne on the flight.'

'I won't.' Bethany sniffed and looked shyly at Matthew. 'Thanks for the limo and—and…everything!' She went on tiptoe and gave him a quick kiss on the jaw, which he returned with a continental salute on both her tear-stained cheeks that made her blush.

'It was my pleasure,' he said gravely. 'You're a delightful young woman, Beth…and a credit to all your family.'

His subtle phrasing caused her to give him a sudden look of mature comprehension. 'I guess I'll see you again some time…' she said.

'I guess you will.'

She glanced again at the woman at his side. 'See you, Rachel...'

'See you...'

'You're allowed to cry, you know,' murmured Matthew, as Rachel turned her back on her last glimpse of the pair and walked stiffly away, shoulders squared and jaw clenched, her long legs eating up the broad expanse of terminal carpet. 'It's considered *de rigueur* at airports.'

'I'm not going to cry,' she denied.

She got into the back of the limo and slid across to the far window, leaving a wide expanse of leather seat between them. As the limo purred back into the flow of traffic she kept her head turned to stare with fierce concentration out of the tinted window. After a few kilometres of thick silence she heard a soft rustle, and a white handkerchief appeared on the edge of her blurry vision.

'Thank you, but I have some tissues somewhere...' Her sight almost totally obscured by her silent stream of tears, she wrestled with the catch on her bag until suddenly it was wrenched out of her hands and thrown onto the opposite seat.

'Dammit, Rachel, just take it!' He forced his handkerchief into her hand, and she startled them both by suddenly twisting her body around and throwing herself against his shoulder in a paroxysm of noisy sobs.

He had unclicked his seat belt to draw near, and now he undid hers so that he could wrap his arms around her trembling torso and hold her more tightly against his warm chest, uttering soothing reassurances as she wept into his jacket.

'It's OK, it's OK,' he murmured, patting her back, his chin resting on top of her ruffled head. 'You have a right to cry...'

'I'm always saying goodbye. Everyone always leaves…'

'I'm not leaving. I'm right here. And your daughter is moving on to a new phase of her life, but she'll still be your daughter wherever she is…' She was shaken by a renewed storm of sobs. 'That's right, let it all out…'

She did, in a series of disjointed little rushes, punctuated with fresh tears.

'It isn't as if I haven't already let go…I did that when she was born…before that, even. I—my parents didn't want to know about the baby—they even tried to stop Robyn adopting her. But she knew I hated the idea of losing touch completely, and she so badly wanted a child herself…it seemed like fate. And then, just after Beth was born, Simon was posted to Hong Kong for six years.'

'Oh, darling…'

She hastened to dismiss his shocked pity. 'No, no—it was better that way; it was the exactly right thing to happen.' She hiccuped between sobs. 'It would have been too confusing otherwise. The clean break gave Robyn and Beth a chance to really bond as mother and child, and it gave me a chance to grow up. So by the time they came back to New Zealand to live Beth *was* just like a real niece to me—someone I loved, but more as an indivisible part of Simon and Robyn than as a part of me…you know what I mean…?' She was aware of Matt nodding against the curve of her scalp. 'It all seemed so natural, and Beth was so secure that she never had any problem knowing that I was the one who gave birth to her. I've *never* regretted it…not really—' She choked. 'Robyn is such a terrific mum.'

He cupped her chin and tilted her face up to his so that she couldn't hide her expression. 'And I bet *you* will be too,' he told her quietly.

His soft words dropped into the hollow of her heart.

'I'm nearly thirty-one!' she pointed out, her hazel eyes brimming.

'Oh, dear—then you'd better make sure you take a younger lover, with plenty of lusty enthusiasm and stamina,' he murmured, looking down into the deep V of her dress, where her ripe breasts nestled in mouth-watering splendour. 'What a coincidence there's someone on hand who happens to meet the specifications.'

His mouth came down on hers, smothering her squeak of outrage that he should make such a mockery of her pain, but she was swiftly appeased by the steamy pleasure of his soul-deep kisses. His arm tightened around the back of her waist and she angled her mouth against his to give him even greater access, crushing the lapels of his jacket in her eager hands. Her tears dried up completely, her aching awareness of loss replaced by a sense of straining fullness, the temperature in the air-conditioned back seat steadily rising as the limo wound its way back across town.

When Rachel resurfaced, conscious of the sudden cessation of engine vibration, she was aghast to find herself plastered astride Matthew's lap; his hands were burrowed inside her halter, his head thrown back against the headrest, his parted mouth wet with her kisses, his eyes behind his fogged spectacles shut tight and his face drawn into a rictus of agonised restraint.

'Just—don't move for a moment,' he instructed in a stifled voice.

Glancing out of the window, Rachel saw she was back home, and felt a traitorous stab of disappointment as she ignored his plea, pushing away his hands and scrambling frantically off his lap, lunging for the door.

She nearly fell out of the car in her eagerness to alight, and dashed up the path, only to pull up short at the front door when she realised she didn't have her keys.

She turned and found Matthew, walking with preternatural care, bringing her her bag and the gauzy jacket she had shed some time on the feverish return journey.

He had smoothed down his wildly disordered hair but his eyes still had a hectic glitter behind the silver frames.

Rachel had intended to shut the door in his face, but he was on her heels as she stepped inside, and instead of taking him to task she froze, a prickle running down her spine, her senses swiftly changing focus.

CHAPTER EIGHT

RACHEL frowned, and began a swift prowl of the rooms.

Matthew, alert to every nuance of her expression, stuck close. 'What's the matter?'

It took her a little while to figure out why she was getting a feeling of wrongness. 'Someone's been here in the house while we've been gone.'

'Are you sure?'

Rachel adjusted a file on the desk in the corner of the lounge. 'Things have been moved, doors left in a different position...'

'Maybe Robyn or Beth—'

'No. I rechecked the whole house before we left and I have an excellent visual memory.' She pushed in a drawer of the desk that wasn't quite closed and shivered. 'Nothing too overt, but someone's definitely been in here, going through my things. I know it. I can *feel* it.'

He didn't deride her intuition, as Frank would have done. Instead he insisted she go through the house with him again, pointing out the subtle evidence, discovering the slight rearrangement of clothing in her drawers. 'Whoever it was has done a very neat job,' he commented. 'Can you tell if anything is missing?

'There doesn't seem to be,' she said, nibbling her lower lip and finding it embarrassingly tender. 'There's no sign of a forced entry-point, either, so it's not a run-of-the-mill B&E; it has to have been a skeleton-key job...'

'You don't have an alarm?' He frowned.

She shrugged. 'We don't get much crime in this area—

it's a friendly neighbourhood—and, anyway, I don't have a great deal of stuff worth stealing—the computer, the microwave and video are usually first to go in a burglary, but it looks as though they haven't even been touched.'

'Probably not a burglary, then. Someone looking for something else? Do you keep any of Westons' security-sensitive stuff here?'

'Certainly not—Frank's very strict about that kind of thing.'

'What about this mysterious harasser Robyn was talking about? Could he or she have turned to stalking?'

'It simply doesn't fit the pattern—all the other things have been impersonal ways of getting at me from afar, without running any risk of a face-to-face confrontation.'

'Then what *is* worth someone running that sort of risk for?'

The thought struck them both at the same time, and Rachel rolled away her computer chair and hauled out her briefcase, which she had shoved to the back of the tunnel under her desk.

'The photographs—' she said in dismay when she knelt down and unsnapped the case. She sat back on her haunches. 'They're gone!'

Matthew swore. 'So it could very well have been our blackmailer.'

'But no one knew I had them! Except *you*...'

His eyes kindled. 'Are you accusing me of paying someone to toss over your house while we were making out on the back seat of my Dad's car?'

His phrasing was deliberately designed to make her blush, but she refused to give him the satisfaction. 'No, of course not,' she said weakly, rising back to her feet.

'I know you don't really trust me yet, but at least credit me with *some* sense of morality,' he scolded her, before turning back to the immediate problem. 'Since our engagement was announced maybe whoever it is needs to urgently find out what's *really* going on between us. And, since my residences are pretty well impregnable, the logical place to troll for stray information on our relationship would be here. The fact part of the evidence has been retrieved might indicate our blackmailer is getting cold feet. Thank God you keep that unfortunate note I wrote to you close to your heart—'

'It's in my *wallet*,' she corrected him sharply.

He grinned. 'I was speaking figuratively,' he soothed.

'Well, there was nothing else to be found, so I doubt whoever it is will come back,' murmured Rachel, wrapping her arms around her waist. The late afternoon was edging into evening, and soon she would have to start thinking about her solitary meal. She lifted her chin. She probably wouldn't feel like anything much after their superb four-course lunch. Maybe just a boiled egg in front of the TV...

Matthew was observing her contradictory body language. 'Not that it matters, because, friendly neighbourhood or not—you're not staying here,' he announced. 'Not tonight, anyway. And preferably not until we arrange to have the locks changed and a decent alarm installed.'

Rachel tossed her head, her eyes flaring with pride. 'I'm not scared!'

'Maybe not, my dear lioness, but *I* am,' he said with rueful truth. 'If anything happened to you I'd feel responsible, and I have enough on my conscience. I'm not prepared to leave you here alone, Rachel, and that's that! And if you're honest you'll admit you don't really want to be by yourself tonight, either. You're staying with me.'

Honesty hadn't had a hell of a lot to do with allowing herself to be persuaded into his unnecessarily protective custody, Rachel thought to herself later, as she lay in a huge bath of bubbles in one of the upstairs bedrooms of his country fortress. The real truth was that she had craved more of those mind-blowing kisses, and in that she had been severely disappointed for Matthew had suddenly become as virtuous as a priest.

After entertaining her with a detailed tour both inside and outside his house that would have done credit to the impersonality of a real estate salesman, Matt had urged Rachel to have a swim while he prepared another of his delicious light salads, this time with shrimp, for their evening meal. He had served it with a crisp white wine and kept the conversation innocuous, and then, leaving the dishes in the sink for the housekeeper to deal with the next morning, had pleaded pressure of work and gone through a stack of papers while Rachel had curled up on the other end of the couch and tried to concentrate on a borrowed book, sipping her way through another glass and a half of wine.

She had felt all her senses humming by the time he had closed the last folder, only to find herself confronted by a masculine yawn and a polite goodnight that had shunted her off to her room...alone. There her thoughts had grown oppressively melancholy, until she had banished them by mentally weaving a series of passionate fantasies which she now had an urgent desire to turn into reality.

Stepping out of her bubble bath and patting herself dry on the huge dark green bathsheet, Rachel reached for the sexy knee-length white satin chemise that Robyn had given her as a thank-you present that morning. It had looked quite modest in the box, but, looking at herself in the mirror, she realised that the slinky fabric concealed yet cleverly revealed the peaks and valleys of her body, sliding against her skin with every breath, the tips of her breasts showing as sharp points against the pearly satin.

She smoothed down the sides with trembling hands, a

little tingle shooting through her as her fingers encountered her silky thighs through the daring slits that reached almost to her hip. She had had just enough wine to free her from nervous inhibition, and more than enough to dispel any niggling fear of rejection. She ached with a deep-seated need that Matt was destined to appease.

He hadn't told her where his own room was—a glaring omission which Rachel refused to consider a deterrent. Her feet bare, she embarked on her quest through the maze of quiet, carpeted hallways on the upper floor, her figure shimmering like a ghost in the pale rays of the silver moon which shone down through the strips of patterned glass in the ceiling.

When she finally saw the mellow glow of an electric light spilling out through a half-open door, Rachel ventured in without knocking.

'You said I wouldn't want to be by myself tonight, and you were right...'

Matt, clad only in his cream trousers, his belt unbuckled, whirled around from the low mirrored bureau, his unshielded eyes flaring with shock. He threw the towel he was holding onto the dark-covered bed and strode towards her.

'Dammit, Rachel, what are you doing here?' His voice was hoarse as his gaze slid over the waterfall of satin to focus briefly on the rippling V where her thighs met before racing back up to her face. Even without his glasses he could still recognise trouble when he saw it. 'If I'd already turned on the motion sensors the security board would be lit up like a Christmas tree right now!'

'But you hadn't. You knew I might be lonely,' she said huskily, and reached out to walk her fingers up his naked chest. 'You told me I shouldn't be alone tonight...'

He caught her wrist. 'Don't do that,' he ordered roughly.

'Why not?' With her other hand she touched his flat nipple. It was hot, dry and beaded instantly under her touch. She felt a surge of reckless pleasure. 'Isn't this what you expected when you brought me here?'

'For God's sake.' His fingers manacled both her wrists, holding them out to her sides. 'Not now, not like this...'

'Like what?' she asked, moving forward so that the front of her thighs brushed his and her satin-tipped breasts settled against his skin. She bent her knee, excited by her own daring, allowing it to nudge between his muscle-locked legs. She lifted her face and touched her tongue to the ridge of his jaw, tasting his tangy male flavour.

'When?' she murmured seductively. 'When will you make love to me, Matt?' The lighting was sensuously low, and the simple functionality of the room spurred her imagination. 'I want you to love me here, now...on the bed, on the bureau, on the floor—I don't care,' she purred. 'I just know we can make each other feel good...'

'Rachel—' He groaned as she tasted him again, sipping and nibbling at the dark stubble on his chin, pushing closer and rubbing herself wantonly against his stiff body. 'Dammit, I promised myself I wasn't going to let this happen,' he gritted. 'I should never have let you drink the rest of that wine, but I thought it might help you relax...'

'I'm relaxed,' she whispered against his mouth, insinuating her leg further between his. 'I'm not drunk, I know what I'm doing...'

'It's night, your biorhythms are low, your emotional defences are down...and you're missing the people you love,' he said raggedly, pulling his reluctant mouth away from her kiss. 'The feel-good bit is just an illusion—it won't last the dawn. You don't really want sex, you want love, and you don't really want *me* to love you; you just want to be close to someone—*anyone*—who can fill the emptiness for a while. Don't think I'm not tempted,' he grunted, jerking his hardening body away from her sinuously stroking hips. 'But I won't be used as an emotional substitute—not ever again. I've been used like that once before, and it was sheer hell...'

He shuddered, drawing her hands together, binding them in an attitude of prayer as he pressed them to his lips. 'I want you to trust me, not resent me for taking advantage of your vulnerability.'

Rachel shook her head fiercely. 'You wouldn't be taking advantage. Do you think I don't know the difference between seduction and force? I know what it's like to be *truly* forced.' She spoke feverishly in her effort to convince. 'That's how Bethany was conceived. I was raped by a drunk—the father of a boy I'd started dating. At first I was too scared and too ashamed to tell anyone, and then I found I was pregnant.

'It turned out that he'd raped other girls, too, even younger than me, and there was a court case during which he died. I was glad! I hated him for what he did, and it took me a long time to learn to trust men again. It also made me very selective about with whom I chose to be sexual.' She swayed against him. 'So if you're my choice then I *must* trust you...'

'Oh, no—oh, God, Rachel...' Matt's eyes were smouldering coals in a face which was suddenly ash-grey. 'I never imagined— I'm so *sorry*...' His voice was racked with a deep torment that seemed to go beyond empathy.

'I had Bethany,' she said, as if it explained her survival, and in many ways it did. 'What goes wrong in our lives doesn't always turn out to be all for the worst.' Desire made her impatient. 'Anyway, what does it matter *why* we want each other tonight?'

'It matters.' He looked painfully shaken, the barrier of

his will breached by her honesty, but not broken. 'I can't
do this casually. I—Leigh was the first woman I ever
loved.'

'I know that—'

'No, you *don't* know. No one really knows how it was
with Leigh!' He turned away to pace the room, punching
his words out in jagged phrases. 'I had—I was extremely...introverted and awkward around girls as a teenager, but she lived just up the road from us and was kind
to me whenever our paths crossed. From the age of seventeen I was wildly in love with her. At least, I thought it
was in the cause of love I was keeping myself chaste and
true, but now I wonder whether it was just infatuation, intensified by the fact that she encouraged my emotional at-
tachment but kept me physically at arm's length. Then I
introduced her to my cousin, and she fell for him like a ton
of bricks.'

'Neville?' The spiky relationship between the two men
was suddenly explained.

His head jerked in assent. 'Even when I knew they were
sleeping together I was still tied up in knots about her. I
stayed faithful to her on the strength of our friendship, in
the hope that one day she'd realise that it was me she actually loved. Neville didn't have a good track record with
women. Whenever they had a row she'd run to cry on my
shoulder, and I'd beg her to give him up and marry me—'

'And one day she said yes,' supplied Rachel tentatively,
wondering where these raw revelations were leading.

'Oh, yes, she married me—in a fit of despair and pregnant with Neville's baby.' He ran a hand through his hair,
his voice sounding unutterably weary. 'Leigh was a nurse—
she'd tested positive for HIV after a needle-stick accident,
and when Neville found out he couldn't handle it and
dumped her. He was terrified of the idea of being infected,

or being stuck with a partner with full-blown AIDS, and when she told him she was pregnant he told her to have an abortion. So Leigh finally took me up on my offer. I was young and arrogant enough to think myself her gallant saviour, but she never stopped loving Neville long enough to try and build any sort of real life with me. She was so traumatised by the way she'd lost him she took on his attitude as a kind of self-punishing obsession.'

The long muscles of his arms rippled as he bunched his fists at the memory. 'She went ahead with an abortion without telling me and then decided that I was far too good for her and that she had no right to my love. She'd always been emotionally delicate, but she became an obsessive-compulsive, constantly cleaning the house and herself, afraid that she was going to accidentally contaminate somebody else. Her HIV status never changed, but she was convinced she was tainted, unworthy of being happy. She was a nurse, and intellectually she knew that HIV isn't the sentence of doom it once was, but she still couldn't exercise any control over her fears without the help of tranquillisers. Do you know what she wrote in her suicide note? That sometimes just to live is an act of courage, and that hers had all dwindled away...'

'Oh, Matt...' Rachel's throat ached to find the words to ease his pain. When she had researched his background she had read the initial news report of Leigh Riordan's death, which had included a reference to Leigh being Matt's 'childhood sweetheart' and a wedding photo of a slender and fine-boned bride, wearing a gamine smile and looking ethereally young in her fairytale gown. At her side twenty-year-old Matt had appeared touchingly grave in comparison.

'I was only ever a substitute to Leigh, and obviously a poor one at that,' he continued choppily. 'She certainly found no solace in my arms, because she wouldn't let me touch her for most of our marriage, let alone ever make love to her—no matter what precautions I offered to take...'

She had been bracing herself for him to admit that he was also HIV positive, and now Rachel sucked in a sharp breath. 'You mean...?'

He stopped his pacing and stared directly into her stunned eyes. 'I mean that our marriage was never consummated.'

'I—I see...'

'I don't think you do. One way or another—through love, loyalty, or guilt over her death—Leigh has kept me celibate since the tender age of seventeen.' He paused as her hazel eyes widened even more, her lips parting in disbelief. 'The very, *very* tender age...' he drawled significantly.

Rachel felt hot and cold and dizzy, all at the same time. 'I—what exactly are you saying?'

He rubbed his bare chest with slow, distracting strokes. 'Exactly? That far from being the accomplished lover my behaviour so far may have encouraged you to believe, my practical sexual experience is virtually nil. I've never been anyone's lover.'

Rachel tore her attention away from his chest and took an involuntary step back, crossing her arms across her breasts to hug herself in thunderstruck confusion. 'But I...you—'

'Don't worry.' He interrupted her babble with a wry smile that made her even more flustered. 'Virginity isn't catching.'

Virginity? His? This lean, sexy, hard-bodied man she had been fantasising so lustily about was still a *virgin*? Colour poured into Rachel's face as she felt her body react helplessly to the notion, her nipples peaking against her shielding arms and darting thrills radiating through her lower extremities.

'Shouldn't *I* be the one blushing?' he asked, and indeed there was high colour streaking along his cheekbones as he watched her struggle with the arousing concept of his innocence.

'I had no idea...' she murmured inanely.

'I do try and keep that kind of information out of the public domain,' was his dry reply. 'Virginity is not something for which a mature man is traditionally admired. My enemies would have a field-day with their jokes.'

He put his hands on her bare shoulders, toying with the shoestring straps of the chemise. 'Seeing you in this erotic piece of confection excites me,' he admitted huskily. 'I very much want to make love with you. But I wanted you to know why it's so important to me that there not be any mistake about what you're really feeling. You need to know what you're taking on when you invite me to be your lover. I don't want my first time with a woman to be a one-night stand or a casual fling. For once in my life I want the woman of my desiring to come to me freely—from joy, not from sorrow...'

She bit her lip, torn between fear of the tumultuous emotions his words had aroused and the wild passion urging her to throw caution to the winds and take what she wanted—and worry about having to pay for it later.

Instead of disappointing him, her gnawing teeth, softly furrowed brow and slightly resentful gold stare brought a sultry amusement to his gaze. He smoothed his hands over her elbows and down to the wide swell of her hips, applying enough firm pressure to turn her around to face the way she had come.

'Of course, I expect the sex to be utterly spectacular when we *do* get together,' he murmured in her ear as he gently propelled her to the door, his warm hand curving on her rounded bottom for a final farewell pat. 'So remind me to make sure those motion sensors are switched off; otherwise, when the earth moves for us, we'll have a squad of policemen thundering into our bedroom!'

CHAPTER NINE

RACHEL was given no chance to suffer any morning-after awkwardness from the night before.

Surprisingly, considering the state in which she had finally gone to bed, she had slept dreamlessly and well, to be woken next morning by the kiss of dark-roasted coffee on her nostrils. Opening her eyes, she saw Matt, breakfast tray in hand, sitting himself down on the side of her bed. As she struggled upright against the luxurious stack of fluffy pillows behind her he leaned over to place the light silver tray across her lap.

'Good morning!' he said with shattering cheerfulness.

Still dazed with sleep, Rachel looked down at the crisp strips of curling bacon and a sunny egg, surrounded by triangles of wholemeal toast and garnished with a yellow rosebud. A glass of orange juice stood beside the gently steaming coffee cup. She couldn't remember when she had last been offered the luxury of breakfast in bed.

'I can't eat all this,' she protested automatically, tucking the silk sheet modestly across her breasts.

'I'll help.' Matt casually hitched up the drooping left shoulder-strap on her chemise, and, smiling into her slumberous eyes, filched a piece of bacon, crunching into it with his strong white teeth.

'Did you cook this?' she asked, picking up her fork, trying not to notice how sexy he looked in pale blue jeans and a crisp, white cotton shirt open at the throat. She was in danger of getting sex on the brain!

'Sara did—my housekeeper,' he said. 'I had something

earlier—but I've worked up a whole new appetite waiting for you to wake up.' Her fork clattered against her plate as his not-so-innocent smile invited her to speculate on which particular new appetite he had in mind. 'Eat up. We have a busy day ahead of us.'

'We do?' Had he guessed she might wake up with cold feet, appalled by the way she had thrown herself at him?

'Well, a single announcement doesn't an engagement make, you know. If we want to persuade people we're a genuine couple we have to *act* like a proper couple. Fortunately, I've never been flamboyant enough to be of interest to the popular press. My PR man had to offer a serious bribe to get that little titbit about us in yesterday's paper. So if the photos *do* surface I don't think even the tabloids will work up any enthusiasm about some boring businessman's faked-up cavortings with his fiancé...'

Rachel knew when she was being distracted. 'What do you mean, *act* like a couple...?' she asked dubiously.

She found out over the next few days, as all her spare time was reassigned to support the notion of their 'whirlwind courtship'.

First was their Sunday visit to the hospital, where Rachel had to suffer the embarrassment of being fussed over by Dorothy Riordan, who chided her son for having been in too much of a rush to even buy a ring for his new fiancé.

'She couldn't decide which one she wanted,' he lied with a grin. 'She's a hard woman to please.'

'That's not true, Mrs Riordan,' Rachel defended herself vigorously. 'Matt didn't even bother to *ask* me to marry him. He simply *announced* it to the world!'

There—that had wiped the smirk off his face!

Instead of looking properly disapproving, the other woman was amused by her son's sudden chagrin.

'Did he really? What a coincidence—his father did much

the same thing when he met me. I must say, it did make for a very exhilarating courtship,' she added reminiscently, observing the crackling tension between the pair. 'As I told you the other day, my dear…Matt can be annoyingly *managing*…'

'I call it being masterful,' he said, to which Rachel answered with an inelegant snort.

'I haven't mentioned it to your dad yet, darling…you know what he's like,' the sprightly lady warned Matt as he prepared to look in on his father. 'I think we'd better leave it until safely after his operation tomorrow, don't you? He's bound to get excited. He still has that crazy bee in his bonnet about…' She nudged Matt aside and lowered her voice to a stage whisper which was clearly audible to Rachel's burning ears. 'About you and *you know who*…'

Matt patted his mother's shoulder with a chuckle. 'It's OK, Mum, Rachel knows all about Cheryl-Ann. And she's more than capable of standing up to Dad if he tries to cut up rough. She might not have the social pedigree he's been touting for, but she has far more enduring qualities. She has the heart of a lion, the strength of an Amazon, the compassion of an angel…all wrapped up in the most gorgeous body I've ever seen!'

'You didn't have to lay it on so thick,' muttered Rachel afterwards. 'You made me sound like a cross between Joan of Arc, Wonderwoman and a Playboy bunny! I hate deceiving your mother like this; she's going to be so hurt when she finds out this is all a pack of lies.'

'Why should she? If our engagement doesn't end up at the altar she'll be disappointed for me, but I know she'd prefer to see us break up than for me to go through another wretched marriage.'

If…? Not *when*? Rachel wondered whether to challenge him on his use of words as he continued,

'I don't want to add to her burden of worry about Dad by telling her my troubles. At least I've been able to find out that Dad never looked at his private mail the day of his heart attack—thank God! With luck our engagement will be all the disincentive our malicious ill-wisher needs to persuade him he's flogging a dead horse...'

To that end, their next visit was to a jeweller's, where Matt told the obsequious salesman that his main requirement was that his fiancé's ring be 'big and bold'.

'Now he thinks you're crass,' murmured Rachel as she left the store with what felt like a huge weight dragging on her finger.

'Nonsense, darling. He only has to look at you to realise what beauty there is in opulence.' To the amusement of passers-by he smothered her huff with a kiss to which she recklessly responded, quieting her conscience by telling herself that she was just playing a part.

'I thought something dainty and small would be all wrong for your hands,' he said, taking her hand as they walked to the Porsche. 'I like this one because it's so unashamedly different. That beaten gold gives it a lovely, barbaric look, don't you think? Like something an Amazon queen might have worn...'

She remembered the strikingly eccentric pieces of art in his house and looked again at the flash of fire on her ringfinger, seeing it not only with her eyes but with her heart. He could have chosen something bland and generic to go with the pretence, but instead he had gone for something that he thought would specifically suit *her*, something eyecatching yet also resonant with a deeper symbolism, a ring that was as sensuous as it was striking.

'I suppose so...' she admitted reluctantly. It wouldn't do for her to fall in love with something that she knew was only on loan.

Like the man himself...

The ring was a big hit with everyone who saw it, and even prompted a generous apology from Frank.

'I'm sorry I blew my top at you the way I did on Saturday,' he told her after their Monday staff meeting, and Rachel waited for him to add the usual rider which would award her partial responsibility for incurring his wrath. Instead he had rambled on about the pressures he was operating under, saying that he hoped he hadn't damaged their working relationship to the extent that she felt unable to confide in him.

Wary of the tension underlying his affability, Rachel stuck to the cover story which she and Matt had agreed upon. To distract Frank from any inconsistencies she told him about the mysterious intruder at the house, stressing that nothing had been taken.

Frank instantly snapped back into professional mode, demanding to know whether she'd called the police.

'I didn't see much point, since nothing was taken.' She shrugged. Seeking to divert him further, she told him about the string of problems she had been having with the council, the post and the tax department. 'But I don't think they're connected with this latest thing...'

'Hmm...why don't I look into it for you?' he offered, with surprising alacrity and none of the stinging criticism she had been prepared to resent. 'It's the least I can do after the way I carried on. Could be that it's related to some case that's gone through here.' He turned to leave her office before swinging back to add as an afterthought, 'Oh, by the way, I've had to let Max Armstrong go.'

'The new man?' Although Frank usually handled dismissals, he normally discussed them with her first. 'You fired him? But I thought you said he was working out quite well.'

'He had a bit of an attitude problem—you know how stroppy those ex-undercover guys can be. With things as financially uncertain as they are right now we have to make extra sure that everyone's pulling their weight. I didn't fire him; I just explained it was a policy of last on, first off...'

Rachel watched him go, vaguely uneasy. Frank never apologised and rarely explained himself, and just now he had done both!

She remembered Matt saying that a doubtful friend was worse than a certain enemy. She had never felt secure in Frank's friendship, and, thinking back to all the times he had played on her sense of inferiority to get his own way, to how he had only incrementally allowed her access to the business and never encouraged personal confidences, her unease deepened. What had suddenly made him so anxious to stand in her trust? Did he think that she might be persuaded to use her new 'influence' with Matt for the benefit of WSS?

Her distaste for the idea made her sharp when Matt rang to make plans for the evening, but she still found herself coaxed into having dinner with his mother and spending another night under his roof, this time in his city apartment.

'But I'm not sleeping with you,' she stated bluntly, not sure who she was punishing most. Since Matt was the cause of her painfully conflicted feelings, she hoped it was him!

Her attempt to reduce his powerful impact on her to its most basic physical—and therefore manageable—level had backfired. Instead she found herself even more deeply ensnared by the attraction, forced to deal with the real man rather than the fantasy, aware that to fulfil his demand for trust would mean surrendering to the frightening emotions he aroused.

As well as a fear of opening herself up to more hurt, Rachel felt intimated by the awesome responsibility he had handed to her: the knowledge that when they made love she would be initiating him into one of the great pleasures of life.

Of course, I expect the sex to be utterly spectacular...

He had only been teasing, but what if she disappointed him? She had enjoyed a good sex life with David, but it had been nothing spectacular, and he had usually been the one to take the lead.

But even when she was back in her house she no longer found it the peaceful haven it had once been. In a startlingly short time Matt had become all-pervasive in her life. At least she had little time to miss Robyn and Bethany, she thought, as she shuttled between the office, the gym and dates with Matt that she was careful to keep confined to public places—although she made no attempt to avoid the passionate kisses on the doorstep which left them both aching and dissatisfied.

His father had come through his by-pass surgery with flying colours, and Rachel was grateful when his doctor restricted visitors to immediate family only for a further few days. She had a feeling that Kevin Riordan was too shrewd to be taken in by the kind of charade which had convinced his wife, and if he asked Rachel flat-out in front of Matt whether she was in love with his son, she feared she didn't know whether the lie she was supposed to admit would also be the truth she was trying to deny.

On the third evening after the operation, Rachel was waiting on the ward for Matt to finish his visit so that they could go to dinner when she was surprised by a familiar voice.

'I understand that congratulations are in order...'

She whirled around to face the tall, handsome man in a pin-striped suit. 'Neville! I didn't know you were back...'

'Not before time, it seems.' Neville's cool grey eyes

were checking out her ring. 'So it's true. I didn't believe that Matthew would risk throwing his hat into the ring again, not when he's still carrying a torch for poor Leigh...'

Rachel didn't think her expression had changed, but the cordial politeness on Neville's flat face congealed.

'Ah, I see he's told you his wife's tragic story. I don't suppose he happened to mention that my mother died of Parkinson's disease? A long, slow degeneration that turned my father into a bitter old man who drank himself to death. I went through hell until I tested free of the Parkinson's gene. I loved Leigh, but I know my own limitations. Sickness disgusts me.' His nostrils flared as he looked around him in distaste. 'I would have been no good to her if she'd got ill. Matt was far better equipped to play the white knight. It was what he'd wanted all along, after all. He still blames me, but how was I supposed to know that Leigh would turn out to be so emotionally unstable?'

Rachel's pity warred with her discomfort. 'I don't think we should be talking about it—'

'Aren't you in the least bit curious to hear the other side of the story?'

'I'm sure Matt will tell me anything I want to know.'

'Are you sure? Oh, he'll tell you everything you could find out from other sources—after all, he knows you run a detective agency—but what about the *really* damning secrets? The ones that *aren't* on any public records...?'

His knowing smile sent a trickle of ice down her spine. 'I really don't think this is the time or place—'

He flicked a glance over her shoulder and picked up her hand. 'Quite right. How about a cosy chat over dinner some time?'

She couldn't believe his audacity. 'No—I—Matt—'

His mouth twisted cynically. 'Lunch, then? Surely he can't object to that?'

'Object to what?' asked Matt, coming up beside them.

Rachel pulled her hand away, flustered when Neville didn't easily let it go.

'Rachel and I were just talking about having lunch. Hope you got my faxes, old boy…thanks for keeping the seat warm for me. How's Uncle Kevin?'

'He's resting,' Matt clipped.

Neville bristled with challenge. 'Are you telling me I can't even see him?'

The two men squared off at each other, then Matt shrugged with impatience. 'Of course not, go ahead—just be aware that he doesn't know about Rachel and I yet…'

'Really? How interesting? *More* family secrets?' Neville's smile was redolent with meaning as he tilted his head towards Rachel and strolled off down the corridor.

Matt turned to Rachel, his eyes stormy. 'He asked you to lunch? Did you accept?'

Rachel was casually dressed in trousers and a cotton sweater, for they were dining at a waterfront café, but she was wearing high-heeled sandals, and now she was glad of the opportunity to coolly look down her nose at him.

'What do *you* think?'

For a moment his narrow face remained tight with fury, then his bunched jaw relaxed. 'I think I'm being unreasonably jealous.'

'Of me, or of Leigh?' she dared.

His darkened eyes moved over her proud face. 'Oh, definitely of you,' he said softly. 'In spite of that stupid, knee-jerk reaction I know you're nothing like Leigh.'

And yet it was Leigh with whom he had fallen so helplessly in love…

She looked in the direction that his cousin had gone. 'Admiration and envy can be quite a poisonous mix. It strikes me that Neville would quite happily cause you trouble if he could. Have you considered that *he* might be behind any attempt at a smear...?'

She found Matt already one step ahead of her. 'I haven't discounted him, though it's not really his style. If the pictures fell into his hands I suppose he wouldn't let the opportunity go to waste, but he'd consider it beneath him to stoop to such methods himself. Nor would he like the idea of being anyone else's tool. His ambitious schemes tend to be more lofty. And I don't see him continuing to target Dad after his heart attack. Apart from the fact he's genuinely fond of my parents, he wouldn't want his spite to reflect back on himself and jeopardise his position in the family. And don't forget he's been in Japan for the past two and a half weeks.'

So...maybe this wasn't a solo effort, she mused. Maybe he had an accomplice. It was an idea worth following up, she thought to herself as they left the hospital.

The next day she had told Matt she was working late at the gym, but to her dismay he turned up far too early to collect her, looking vastly out of place in his dark suit and tie as he propped himself against an exercise bike and watched her chivvy one of her regulars into adding an extra set of reps to her weights programme. The sight of Rachel in stretch shorts and a cropped T-shirt under her cutaway leotard seemed to afford him endless fascination.

'I exhausted myself just watching you,' he murmured, handing over her towel and water bottle at the end of the session, licking his dry lips as he watched her blot the perspiration from her face and throat. 'You stood over that poor woman like a drill sergeant...'

'That "poor woman" is one of the country's leading aerobics competitors. She *pays* me to make sure she doesn't slack off!'

He looked around the gym. 'You work a full day and

then come and do this? And sometimes work in the mornings as well...also at a very physical job? No wonder you nearly fall asleep over dinner some nights.'

He was checking up on her? 'Well, you can't say I'm not fit enough to handle it,' she said, not knowing whether to be flattered or insulted. She flipped the towel over her shoulder, hoping he hadn't noticed her nipples beginning to show through her exercise bra and damp T-shirt. 'Excuse me, I'm going to have a shower.' She made the mistake of looking over her shoulder as she left, and found his eyes fixed on the rolling flex of her bottom in the thin Lycra shorts

Later, as she devoured a chocolate mousse to replace some of the calories she had worked off, he returned to the topic. 'Tell me, Rachel, when do you get any spare time for yourself? I notice Frank Weston doesn't have to moonlight to make ends meet. You shouldn't have to hold down more than one job to survive.'

'And I wouldn't have to if you gave Westons the KR contract,' she said facetiously. She noticed *he* had no problem appropriating her precious spare time! 'How about it?'

'Only if you agree to sleep with me first,' he responded with equal sarcasm.

He was so confident that she was joking! On the one hand it was infuriating; on the other it indicated a complete faith in her integrity.

'Fine! Let's do it!'

She had the pleasure of seeing him winded. 'Fine? What do you mean—*fine*?'

'I accept your offer. It's a deal!'

He recovered quickly. 'You know damned well I don't have the power to do any such deal,' he growled. 'Nor do I want it. Neville's back, thank God—it's his decision. I want nothing to do with it.'

She looked at him through her lashes. 'What if I agree to sleep with you anyway?'

He stilled, staring across the table. 'Do you mean that?'

She hesitated, and nodded.

He let out a rough sigh of pent-up frustration. 'Hold that thought! You do choose your moments, lioness... I'm flying to Sydney on the red-eye tomorrow morning.'

Rachel's reckless heart felt as if it had been plunged into ice.

'Only for a few days,' he added swiftly, and her heart shuddered back into life. 'I've already postponed this meeting twice over the last couple of weeks, and now that Dad is out of the woods I can't put it off any longer. But I'll be back for your birthday.' He leaned forward, placing his hand over hers on the table and gripping it hard. 'I look forward to resuming this discussion when I get back...'

Discussion? What was there left to talk about? A panicked sense of urgency made Rachel wish that he would simply whisk her straight back to his bedroom for a quick consummation, but the knowledge that he would be walking out of the door before dawn put the brakes on her impatient desire. No more than he did she want this first time to be a snatched interlude that would set the scene for future brief encounters. When she made love to him she wanted to do so at leisure, with no distractions, anxieties or interruptions...

The next three days were merely a confirmation of what she had already suspected. They were flat and colourless and she missed Matt more than she would have believed possible. She tried to fill some of the emptiness by putting in overtime at Westons, checking up on Neville, who proved disappointingly clean, and digging into some of the back files that yielded some unexpected and unsettling results.

Matt rang each night for long, lazy chats, but the conversations were inherently unsatisfying as Rachel struggled not to blurt out her newly discovered feelings. It was too late to worry about being hurt, but she wanted to see him, touch him, look into his eyes before she surrendered her wary heart completely into his keeping.

Typically there was only a briefly inscribed card from her parents on her birthday, but there were e-mails, cards and a gorgeous Thai-silk suit from Robyn and Bethany, and at the office she was given a cake and a group-signed card ribbing her about wrinkles.

Having no appointments at the gym, she'd expected the evening to lag as she waited for Matt's flight to get in, secretly hurt by the fact that he had refused her offer to greet his plane. But as she was preparing to leave work Lannie came dashing breathlessly into her office to tell her that a limo driver was asking for her.

Thinking it was one of their security chauffeurs, Rachel was disarmed when she was handed an armful of red roses and a sealed note in memorable green ink.

Go with Kale. He knows what to do. Happy Birthday.

Kevin Riordan's chauffeur professed ignorance as he led her out to the car and placed a glass of champagne in her hand for the mystery ride, but Rachel soon discovered to her amusement and delight that their destination was Auckland's most exclusive beauty clinic. There she was treated to a sinfully sybaritic experience—bathed in mud, wrapped in towels, soaked in a spa, plucked, waxed, massaged in oils, given a facial, a hairdo, a manicure, a pedicure—and generally wallowed in the sensuous luxury of top-to-toe pampering. Like a harem girl being prepared for her master, she thought with a giggle.

She emerged tingling with vitality and filled with a glorious sense of physical well-being that increased when Kale informed her that his instructions were to take her home to change and then on to Matt's country house for dinner.

Matt's face, as he opened the door and saw her standing there in her new peacock-blue silk suit, her glowing cheeks flushed with excitement and her hazel eyes alight with warm pleasure, reassured her that she was making the right decision. This man was not one she wanted to let get away!

'Happy Birthday. You look even more gorgeous than I remember,' were his first words, his glittering gaze taking in the short, narrow skirt and fitting, short-sleeved jacket with its stand-up collar and an array of tiny silk toggles marching down her front.

'Thanks to Robyn—she sent me this,' husked Rachel, fiddling nervously with a toggle under his wildly flattering gaze. In blue-black trousers and shirt, his hair still damp from a shower, he made her knees weak. 'And thanks to you. It was a wonderful present. I've never been to a beauty spa before; it was a totally new experience...'

The flames leapt in his eyes at her gratifying admission. His arm snaked around her waist and he pulled her inside, kicking the door shut on the world as his mouth came down on hers. 'I'm glad. I want to give you lots of wonderful new experiences,' he murmured, rediscovering the silky contrast of textures inside her mouth.

As she followed him through to the room where he had first entertained her she noticed him discreetly rotating his left shoulder and wincing.

'What's the matter with your arm?'

'The taxi was involved in a slight accident on the way to Sydney airport.'

'My God, were you hurt?' asked Rachel anxiously.

'I just jolted my shoulder against the seat belt. Actually,

I think the stiffness is more a build-up of tension from having to use my laptop exclusively for the last few days…'

All the blood rushed to Rachel's head. 'Why don't you let me help you with that?' she heard herself say.

'Help me how?' he said, crossing to the cabinet on which an ice-bucket now reposed.

'Give you a massage…for your shoulder,' she said steadily.

He halted and turned. His chest rose and fell under the dark shirt. 'Are you offering to take my pain away?'

She moved closer, deliberately taking his words at face value. 'If you're over-tense it's the perfect way to ease your muscles into relaxing—I should know; I've just had one myself. Of course it means putting yourself in my hands—'

'I rather think I've done that already.'

'But I *am* fully trained.'

His nostrils flared, the skin on his face tightening as his eyes fell from her lustrous eyes to her smudged lips and her silk-sheathed breasts. I—dinner is almost ready,' he said reluctantly.

She had never felt less hungry in her life. 'Is it anything that can't wait?'

'You mean like a soufflé?' His sultry smile was crooked. 'No, nothing that can't wait…all night long, if necessary.'

Her smoke-coloured eyelids drooped. 'It might well take all night…if you're especially stiff…'

His face flushed. 'I'm sure I'm going to be a very difficult and demanding case…' he murmured thickly. He looked around the room. 'Where do you want to do it? The couch?'

She shook her head as she tried to tamp down her excitement. 'Too soft—not enough support.' She pretended to consider the other furniture in the room before turning her golden gaze to his. 'The bed in your room looked fairly firm…'

She saw his hard throat move as he swallowed. 'Yes, it is.'

'Well, then…' She held out her hand with a glittering smile. 'Shall we go?'

'Just a moment.' He snagged the ice-bucket containing a bottle of champagne and two glasses. 'In case we get thirsty,' he told her as he took her hand, and fairly raced her up the stairs.

'The way you're jostling it, that champagne is going to fizz over when you try to open it,' she warned as they arrived breathless in his bedroom.

'That makes two of us,' he muttered under his breath as he set the ice-bucket down beside the bed and switched on the lamps. He removed his spectacles and swung eagerly towards her. 'Now what?'

She moistened her lips. 'Now you take off your shirt. Have you got any lotion I can use?'

'I'll have a look.' He walked towards the bathroom, dragging open his buttons as he went.

'In fact, take all of your clothes off,' ordered Rachel daringly as he clicked on the light. 'It'll be more comfortable for you that way.'

There was no sound from the bathroom for long moments, and she was about to investigate when he stepped out.

She sucked in a shaky breath. He was wearing nothing but a small white towel wrapped low on his lean hips, pulling tightly across his strong thighs and exposing a vertical strip of bare skin where the two ends only just overlapped. He stood for a moment, letting her look her fill, revelling in her smoky-eyed approval. Then his muscles meshed smoothly into motion, his skin gleaming like dull satin in the lamplight, as he prowled towards her and handed her a slim bottle of skin moisturiser, and something else.

'You might find some use for this, too,' he said, wrapping her fingers around the small foil packet.

She blushed when she opened her hand and saw what it was. 'I—yes, I probably will,' she stammered.

'You started this game, honey,' he purred. 'Maybe you're not quite as brazen as you want me to think you are.'

She tossed her head and strode to the bedside, placing the condom down beside the bottle of champagne. With a flourish she ripped back the navy covers and threw them to the bottom of the bed. 'Face down on the bed, please.'

He paused with one knee on the edge of the mattress, putting the towel to indecent strain and revealing a flash of dark hair against the pale skin of his groin. 'As I recall, the last time you invited me to have a massage I ended up tied to the bed.'

'Lie down, please,' she said sternly, sliding a pillow under his shoulders as he settled on his stomach, his face turned towards her on the white sheet.

Her hands went to the zip at the back of her waist and she watched the ripple of tension invade his entire body. 'What are you doing?'

'I don't want to get any lotion on my new skirt.' She took it off and placed it—neatly folded—on the bureau.

He gave a tortured groan when she strolled back to stand by the head of the bed. 'You wicked *tease...*'

She smoothed a finger down the white lace suspender that secured her gauzy stocking, and back up to the high-cut side of her white silk thong. 'Not at all. It's a matter of practicality,' she lied. 'Stockings are much cooler than pantyhose in the summer.'

'What about your top?' he said slyly. 'You don't want to get lotion on that, either.'

'I think I'll leave that on...for now.' She poured lotion on her hands and stroked them together in front of his fascinated gaze, hoping he would not notice that they were trembling.

Instructing him to fold his arms out to his sides, she leaned over and placed her hands against the nape of his neck, just below the occipital bone. It didn't take her long to identify the congested bands of muscle, and she began to use long strokes to create a deep friction that made him moan with pleasurable pain. Progressing slowly over his back with a gradually increasing pressure, she bent into her work, enjoying the sensuous slide of her thumbs as they dug into the pressure points and worked out the tightness on either side of his spine.

'Oh, God, that feels good!' he muttered.

'I haven't even *begun*,' she promised throatily, her hand going to his towel.

He tensed as she dragged it off, and uttered a hiss of shock as she climbed onto the bed, straddling his naked thighs and beginning to knead his clenched buttocks, hooking her strong fingers deeply into the gluteal muscles. He buried his face in the sheet, uttering another groan, his arms contracting around the pillow under his chest.

She admired him with her hands as well as her eyes, free to gloat over her enticing prize. He was so wonderfully, indisputably *male*, his skin so fine-grained as it curved over the flexing muscle, and lightly dusted with a mist of dark hair that vanished into the intriguing crease between his buttocks. She traced it lightly with one very unprofessional finger.

Sweat broke out on his back. 'Oh, God, Rachel, what are you doing to me...?'

'Shh,' she murmured, as she pushed the heel of her hand against the swell of his buttock and began to rock against his hip with her full weight. 'I think you have some serious chronic tension here…let me see what I can do to relieve it…'

'I can tell you, you're making it ten times worse!' he groaned as she continued to stroke him, compressing his hips rhythmically into the bed. 'Much more of this and I'm in danger of exploding like that champagne bottle!'

He reared up when he felt the warm press of lips in the hollow at the base of his spine and the moist flick of a tongue. 'I bet that's not in any damned massage manual,' he gasped.

'It's in *my* manual,' murmured Rachel, propping herself over him on her hands and knees as she kissed her way slowly up his long spine. 'My love manual,' she teased. 'Turn over,' she whispered in his ear, before easing aside to let him make the move.

'I hope you're prepared to take the consequences,' he said, rolling boldly onto his back. His colour was high, his eyes challenging as he watched her assess the bold thrust of his manhood, jutting from the dark fur in his loins.

'Oh, yes…' Rachel felt a gush of heat between her legs. With a rough sound Matt grabbed her by the arms and pulled her down against his chest.

'Aren't you going to finish what you started?' he demanded, dragging her thighs on either side of his and wedging her tight against the thrusting boldness. He slid his hand up into her hair and tugged, guiding her mouth down to his, biting kisses against her soft lips as he said harshly, 'I love the feel of your hands on me…your mouth…your body…everything about you. I want everything you have to give…'

She struggled upright, feeling the thick heaviness of him

butting against the fragile silk thong, aware of the musky scent of his arousal mingling with the sharp fragrance of the lotion she had massaged into his back. She squirmed against him, frantic with excitement, driving herself closer to the very edge of sensual endurance. Her head tipped back, her eyes closing as she stroked his chest, overflowing with love and longing, not caring that she was no longer playing her part. She wanted him, she loved him, she didn't want to wait any longer to make herself irrevocably part of him...

'Isn't it time for you take off your jacket?' he wondered, and she drew his hand to the lowest toggle.

'Here, you do it...'

He was clumsy, too eager. 'These are too little...my hands are shaking like crazy...'

'So are mine.' She showed him, laughing down at him as he fumbled at his task.

He laughed exultantly back. 'You can't be more nervous than I am.' He pulled apart her jacket at last and uttered a choked sound. 'I think I've died and gone to heaven—what *is* this piece of confectionery?' He explored the boning that shaped her body, up to the glory of her breasts, spilling over the top of the frothy lace, the blue veins prominent against the translucence of her skin.

'A basque. It laces down the front, see...'

'Oh, God, more fastenings...' Their fingers tangled together as she impatiently assisted, and as the delicate structure slid away in a tangle of ribbons and lace they both sighed in mutual delight.

'Glorious...all the woman I could ever want...' he murmured, gathering her up in his cupped hands and burying his face in her abundance.

Her hands clasped his head and she cried out as his seeking mouth found her straining nipple and drew on it with hungry fervour, drinking in the richly feminine flavour of her velvety-soft skin.

'Such a delicious mouthful...' He grazed to her other breast, and suckled there, too, drawing out her nipple with his teeth until it throbbed with delicious agony.

She sobbed. 'Matt—'

'What—am I hurting you?'

'No, oh, no—'

'Good...' his mouth surrounded her nipple again, lashing it with his tongue '...because I don't think I can stop...'

His hands reached down to touch the pouting plumpness between her legs. 'Oh, God, you're so wet here...and swollen...' He insinuated his fingers under her thong to torture her with his passionate curiosity, and she twisted frantically so that she could free herself from the last impediment to their lovemaking. As she kicked away the scrap of fabric he shuddered at the settling of her scalding heat against his pulsing erection.

He rolled over on top of her with a hoarse cry, crushing her breasts against his chest as he positioned himself heavily between her thighs, his hair-roughened skin rasping against her smooth stockings. He snatched the small packet from the bedside and cursed as he failed to get it open. In the end Rachel had to do it, but he wouldn't let her help him put the condom on. In a thick voice he told her bluntly that if she touched him like that it would be all over.

The waiting intensified the desire, and soon she was dipping into his mouth again with her tongue, her nails digging into his scalp as she felt his explorative touch parting her intimate folds and his hips jerk as he tested himself against her tight sheath.

'Am I hurting you?'

She felt a delicious stretching, but no pain, and she shook her head on the pillow. Matt raised himself up on one arm, gazing triumphantly down into her passion-blurred face. 'Now…' Looking deep into her eyes, he took her hand and pushed it down between their steamy bodies to cup his virility. 'Show me…take me…' He used her fingers to guide him inside her. 'I want to feel everything you feel. I want it to be you and me, together, every step of the way…' He eased slowly forward, gritting his teeth and shaking with the effort of restraining himself, until she wound her legs around him and deliberately unleashed his most primitive urges, the violent series of penetrating thrusts that shattered their separate selves and fused them into a single, sensual being.

And, true to his naive expectations, the resulting mutual pleasure was utterly spectacular!

CHAPTER TEN

WAKING up next to the man you loved was, Rachel discovered next morning, one of life's most joyous delights. She'd thought Matt had sated himself on his exhaustive exploration of new-found pleasures and would be bound to wake sluggish and heavy-eyed after a long night of vigorous physical activity.

She was wrong.

When her eyes fluttered open he was already lying on his side, propped up on one elbow on the sunlit bed, his gaze bright with curiosity as he watched her lazily shift her shoulderblades against the firm mattress and wake herself with a low, slow stretch that ended in a soft groan at the pleasant pull of aching muscles. Either he or their nocturnal stirrings had pushed the sheet that was their only covering somewhere down around their hips, and he was clearly enjoying the voluptuous visual extravaganza.

'You're insatiable,' she groaned, correctly interpreting the gleam in his eye.

'You're the one who made me that way,' he said with a grin, noticing that she made no effort to draw up the sheets.

'It's rude to watch people while they're sleeping,' she murmured, basking in his admiration.

'I haven't got my glasses on; I can't see a thing,' he lied boldly. He stroked her bare arm where it lay against her side, his knuckles brushing against the relaxed swell of her breast, burnished by a shaft of early-morning sunlight. 'You're very still when you sleep—no shifting, no twitching or sighing…just pure, unadulterated peace.'

163

'Which you've been longing to disturb,' she teased.

'Fair's fair. You've been disturbing *me* just by lying there!' He bent to brush his lips over hers. 'I woke up wanting you.' He deepened the kiss and broke it off slowly, in juicy little bites. 'I woke up imagining that we were still making love, that your gorgeous wet mouth was doing those wicked things to me that made me scream myself hoarse—'

She was suffused by a wave of delicious embarrassment. 'Matt!'

'What? Don't you like to talk about it? You had plenty to say last night. "Not there, Matt!" "Do it like this, Matt".'

Her giggles burst like sweet honey on his tongue. 'I didn't! You didn't seem to need much instruction.'

'Mmm, I was responding to a very basic instinct.' He nibbled down the side of her throat and over the top of her breastbone. 'I obviously have a natural talent for pleasing you.'

'And yourself,' she pointed out, shifting so that her breasts moved enticingly within his area of interest.

'Oh, no, that's entirely your doing.' He blew experimentally on her soft pink nipples, a warm, moist zephyr that caused them to pucker and rise eagerly from the surrounding creamy flesh. He rewarded their jaunty salute to his authority with a soft rain of kisses around the dusky areolae. 'You make love the way you do everything else—with courageous strength and a fiery spirit.'

His ardent praise ignited the passionate sizzle of her senses into a blazing conflagration. 'You mean like this?' she said, kicking away the sheet and rolling over to mash herself against his length.

He growled, and they wrestled across the bed, Rachel somehow ending up easily overpowered and pinned face-down beneath him. He grunted as she arched her spine, pushing her wriggling bottom into his groin.

'Why, you *let* me win, didn't you? You little cheat,' he panted in realisation as she pushed up on her knees, his voice thickening with excitement as he recognised the erotic potential of her submissive position. 'Do you want me to take you like this? Is that it?' he murmured, stroking her bottom and the curvature of her spine with a possessive hand.

He sank his teeth into her shoulder, gently holding her captive as he reached for the replenished supply of protection beside the bed. His chest braced her back, his hands slipping underneath her, one to fondle her swaying breasts, the other to splay across her taut belly, adjusting her to his thrust as he discovered a new and intensely pleasurable thrill to add to his expanding repertoire.

Afterwards he took her in his arms and kissed her damp forehead. 'I thought you might not like the feeling of being sexually dominated like that,' he said, explaining the constraint that he had shown through the dark hours of the night, when he had proved eagerly experimental in most other ways.

She tilted her head back and looked at him with clear eyes. 'You mean because of the rape?'

A painful tautness entered his body, his irises darkening with a haunting uncertainty. 'I know it's not a trauma you'll ever be able to forget or forgive.'

'No, but time is a great healer. I learned that to keep yourself safe doesn't mean to bury yourself out of the way of life.'

Responding to his tender concern, she lay in the safety of his embrace and told him all about the ugliness of the rape, the bitterness it had created with her parents, the pain and joy of bearing an illegitimate child.

She sensed his silent search for words and wondered if she had misinterpreted his compassion. She tried to ease herself out of his embrace. 'But I suppose some people might think I'm tarnished for life—death before dishonour and all that...'

He was swift to disabuse her. 'Oh, no! God, Rachel, no—you can't believe I'd think that of you. Still affected by it, yes—tarnished, *never!*' His hands tightened around her back as he said grimly, 'In fact, if either of us is tainted by the past, it's me—'

Her hand over his lips stopped the words in his mouth. 'Don't. It doesn't worry me that you had a wife with HIV,' she said, assuming he was talking about Leigh. 'You've always been honest with me, and I know you wouldn't put me in danger. I've worked around health professionals—I'm not susceptible to scare mongering.'

'Rachel—'

'The past is the past. It's what we are *now* that matters.' She didn't want to mention the future—that seemed, as yet, too fragile.

'And what *are* we?' He smiled wryly, accepting her philosophy with a mixture of reluctance and bitter relief.

One step at a time, she told herself. 'Why, lovers of course!' she purred.

A ping sounded from the bedside table and she peeped over his shoulder at his electronic watch and sighed. 'I think it's time we got up.'

'I've been up all night,' he said, grinning.

He looked so splendidly cocky he made her laugh. 'I hope you're not going to be this insufferably self-satisfied all day!'

'Of course I'm not; now I have *you* to satisfy me, I don't have to rely on myself,' he said with a leer.

When she swatted him a stinging reproach on his bare

chest he chased her into the shower, which delayed them another half-hour.

Over a rather rushed breakfast, he said, 'You know, watching you at the gym, it occurred to me that we could do with some sort of corporate fitness programme at Ayr Holdings. We have a fully-equipped executive gym, and someone to oversee the equipment, but no one providing expert help or supervised workouts. How about it? Would you be interested in submitting a proposal?'

Rachel stared at him over her coffee. 'Me? But I already have too many jobs, remember?'

'In fact I know quite a few companies that might be interested in sponsoring employee fitness programmes,' he went on. 'It could be the basis of a whole new career for you.'

'I *have* a career: at Westons,' she stressed. 'Why else have I been struggling to learn the trade, working for virtually nothing in an effort to help salvage David's dream—'

'*David's* dream,' he picked up. 'Not yours?'

'Not at first, but now—well, it's opened new doors for me. The work is always challenging, always different.'

'As long as you're sure.'

She drank her coffee. 'You're as bad as Frank. He worries I'm not serious about it, either. Whenever we hit the doldrums he offers to let me bail out if I want to, so I won't be tied to a losing proposition—even though it would be a hardship for him to scrape up the money to purchase my share.'

He studied her thoughtfully. 'That's very generous of him. Ever been tempted to take him up on it?'

'No. I guess he's figured out by now that I'm not a quitter. You wouldn't be making this offer to me because you think it's too downmarket for a tycoon like you to have a girlfriend—'

'Fiancée.'

'—who's a security chick, would you?'

'A *security chick*?' He grinned. 'Is that what they call you on the streets? Is that an updated version of a red-hot mama?'

She turned her nose up at him. 'If you're ashamed of what I do—'

He got up from the breakfast bar and kissed her mouth. 'Of course I'm not. Don't be silly, darling. It was just an idea, that's all. I just want you to be happy.'

'You'll be telling me not to worry my fluffy little head about it next,' she muttered sarcastically, and they both suddenly creased with laughter at the absurdity of the image.

But the disruptive thought returned to trouble her in the heady days that followed, as she fell ever more profoundly in love with the complex man who had brought such unexpected drama and passion into her life.

The emotional intensity of their affair was such that, at times, she believed that Matt's feelings ran as deeply as hers, that even though their love remained undeclared he was as desirous as she to move forward to the next level of intimacy. They talked for hours about almost every aspect of their lives, and made love with impassioned ardour, but at other times Rachel's heightened sensitivity to his moods made her aware of an element of reserve in Matt, a waiting quality that erected an invisible barrier which she was afraid to broach for fear of what lay behind it.

She thought it might be because of his father, who had thrown the expected tantrum when he had been told that his fully-grown son had got himself unofficially engaged to someone who was not on his list of approved political assets. Rachel had weathered her first encounter with the post-operative Kevin Riordan with a gutsy good humour that had gained his grudging respect, but when she taxed Matt afterwards about whether she should stay out of his family's orbit, in order not to create a further rift between father and son, he was adamant in his refusal.

'My love-life is none of his business. Dad never had a hope in hell of breeding me to some dippy debutante and he knows it. He never wanted me to marry Leigh, either…'

Rachel forbore to point out that his father's negative attitude had been fully justified. Even though no one else had been told about Leigh's HIV status, the Riordans couldn't have escaped knowing that her turbulent affair with their nephew had scarcely come to an end before she'd rushed to the altar with Matt.

'He thinks I'm too old for you, as well.' ''Not enough child-bearing years left'' was the delicate way Kevin Riordan had actually put it!

'It's a wonder Mum didn't brain him with his bedpan— seeing she's three years older than him herself!' Matt said wryly. 'He's just blowing smoke in your eyes, Rachel, like he was with all that rot about my shining political future. He knows I have no interest in public office, but it pleases him to pretend to his pals that he's a potential king-maker.'

He took her in his arms and kissed her. 'Stop worrying so much about what other people are thinking. We both know that life is too precious to waste storing up grief for ourselves—let's just enjoy what we have while we have it…'

That sounded ominously like a warning against building castles in the air, and a few days later Rachel's nebulous doubts and fears were given a devastating credibility.

She had arranged to meet Matt after work at his apartment, for which he had given her a key, and, having brought some paperwork to work on until he arrived, she absently answered the phone when it rang instead of leaving the answer-machine to pick up.

It was Neville Stiller, returning a prior call from Matt letting him know that Kevin Riordan was now convalescing at home.

'I didn't know you two had moved in together,' he probed, when Rachel told him that Matt wasn't home.

'We haven't,' she told him coolly.

'We never did get around to having that lunch…'

'No.'

She didn't say anything else, but he had no difficulty in reading her silence. 'And never will, either, huh? Not even as a thank-you to me for giving you that contract you and your partner have been busting your buttons for?'

She didn't like the implication. 'That was a purely business decision on your part, not a personal favour. You should be thanking us for all the money we're going to save KR Industries over the next two years.'

'Does that mean our lunch is on, after all?'

She rolled her eyes. 'Give it up, Neville, you're just trying to use me to get at Matt.'

'Maybe I'm concerned for you? After all, you haven't known him as long as I have—you probably haven't seen the dark side of his personality yet. Anyone who spent time in prison for rape and then had a wife who killed herself is bound to have psychological problems, wouldn't you think?'

Rachel collapsed in the chair by the telephone. 'What did you say?' she whispered in agonised disbelief. 'About his having been in prison?'

'Oops. I suppose that's something that never came up in your conversations. Of course, since he was charged as a minor the information is sealed by the records—so he would have no incentive to tell you, would he? I guess no man likes to admit to a new girlfriend that he served time for raping a fifteen-year-old...'

Rachel hardly heard the rest. Her hand was shaking so badly she dropped the receiver into the cradle and then staggered into the bathroom to be violently sick in the basin.

It couldn't be true; it just *couldn't*, she told her ghastly white face in the bathroom mirror. That would make everything he had told her—everything he was—everything that she loved—a lie!

She looked down at the ring on her finger and shuddered, pulling it off and letting it clatter onto the bathroom cabinet.

The sound of the key in the door of the apartment gave her no time to reorder her splintered thoughts. Nor did she give Matt any time to take her in his arms for their usual greeting.

'Neville called. He said— I— Please, just tell me it's not true?' she pleaded, the instant he walked in the door.

'What isn't true?' Matt asked warily, his eyes on her distraught face as she backed away from his embrace.

'That when you were young you were arrested for raping a girl—a *fifteen-year-old* girl. That you went to *prison* for it?' She put a hand over her mouth to hold in the choked sobs.

To her sick horror Matt didn't leap in with an instant denial. His face was suddenly as white as hers. 'Rachel, it's not what it seems—'

'What it *seems*? Don't tell me how it *seems*—I just want to know if it's true!' she demanded hysterically.

'Rachel, I was going to tell you—'

'*Is it true?*' She screamed. 'It's a simple enough question: were you or were you not charged with rape?'

'Yes, but—'

'And you went to prison?'

'Yes, I was remanded in custody, but—'

'My God...' Tears of shock and misery spurted out of her eyes. She felt as if she had been violated all over again. 'My God, it's all true...'

'No! For God's sake, Rachel, listen to me—*I didn't do it*!'

He reached for her and she backed away, shaking her pounding head. 'I believed you. Like a fool I believed all that stuff about you being a virgin,' she said hysterically, 'a man of honour. I fell in love with you and actually *believed* you...'

Blood darkened his face as he confronted her bewildered horror. 'Then believe me *now*,' he pleaded hoarsely. 'You know I wouldn't lie to you.'

She pressed her hands against her temples. What ghastly irony. Had she fallen in love with a man who had done to another young girl what had been done to her? 'I don't know—I can't think. Why didn't you *tell* me?'

'Because I was afraid. I wanted you to get to know me first, so you wouldn't have any doubts when I told you— so I took the coward's way out...' His desperation turned to a kind of tortured anger. 'For God's sake—I'm in love with you, Rachel, I would never do anything to hurt you! I know I made a mistake not telling you, but is your faith in me really so fragile? You really think I just *pretended* to be sexually inexperienced as part of some sick charade? Believe me—as God is my witness—*I never committed any rape*...'

'I don't know what to believe anymore,' she choked, snatching up her purse. Nausea churned in her belly as she plunged for the door. *Now* he talked about being in love with her? Not in a moment of passion or tenderness, but hitting her with it while she was weak and wounded? And only after she had betrayed her own wretched vulnerability...

'Rachel—'

'No, I have to go. Don't try to follow me—I have to be alone!'

She knew it was dangerous to drive her car in the state she was in, but she didn't care—the homing instinct was paramount: the need to find a place of safety in which to lick her wounds.

Yet before she'd turned thankfully into her own driveway her shocked brain had begun to function again, feeding her the questions that she should have stayed to ask, separating fact from assumption, logical thought from unreasoning emotion.

Think! she urged herself. *Follow the chain of evidence.*

What had Neville actually *said* amongst all that sick innuendo about Matt's 'dark side'?

That Matt had been charged with rape, her memory dredged up. Being charged was very different from being convicted, and surely Neville would have used the stronger word in his accusation if that was the case.

Matt admitted he had been in prison, but he had said he was *remanded*. Remand meant pre-trial.

Matt claimed he had never committed rape.

Given the choice, who would she pick as the more self-serving individual: Neville or Matt?

Which man did she most trust to tell her the truth?

She knew which one she *wanted* to trust, and it was because she had wanted it so very much that she had been afraid to trust her own instincts. That was the crux of her dilemma.

Trust.

All this time she had thought it was Matt holding back on their relationship, but maybe it was really herself who had been waiting for the other shoe to drop. Now it had, and instead of picking it up and inspecting the clue, like a good detective, she had run away.

She had condemned the man she loved without a hearing.

Turning off the engine, she rested her weary forehead on the steering wheel and closed her eyes.

He had been a minor himself at the time. A boy. And he had grown into a man whom she liked and respected...and loved...

A tapping on her window made her jerk her head up, her heart soaring with relief, but it wasn't Matt's face looking in at her.

'Miss Blair? I wonder if I could have a word with you?'

Rachel scrubbed at her salt-encrusted cheeks and fussed around with her bag, waiting for her heartbeat to settle before she got out of the car to face the thin, wiry figure of Max Armstrong.

'What about?' she asked warily, wondering if he was going to berate her for the loss of his job, or plead with her to intercede in getting it back.

After one curious look at her blotched complexion Armstrong said dourly, 'Don't worry, I have no grudge against you—that's why I'm here. I'm off to Aussie, where the pay's better. I just thought I'd better warn you that you might get some aggro down the line from that partner of yours.'

'Frank?'

'Yeah. Remember that high-society party gig we did a few weeks ago...the one with the silver cabinets?'

Merrilyn's! How could she forget? Max Armstrong had been one of two guards dressed as a waiters.

Rachel stiffened against the impending blow. 'Maybe you'd better come inside—'

He wagged his head, his thinning ponytail catching on

the collar of his denim jacket. 'No, thanks. As far as I'm concerned I'm not even here. I just wanted to tell you that Weston asked me to keep you under surveillance that night, to see how you handled things…said he wasn't sure you were up to it and he wanted evidence if anything chancy happened—any sort of stuff-up that could be put down to you. He gave me a camera, one of those new, ultra-low-light, long-lens jobs, and, well…after that guy fell in the pool, I followed you and him to the guest-house…' He tailed off and Rachel tersely picked up the thread.

'You took photos of us?' She didn't need to ask, but she was still struggling to accept that her recent suspicions had yielded bitter fruit.

'Look, it was no big deal as far as I was concerned— but a job is a job. I reeled off a few shots. I don't know how the photos came out, or even if they did, I just handed the camera over to Weston the next day. I told him that there was nothing to it—that you'd had a falling-down drunk on your hands—and he said OK.

'But you were always pretty decent to me, and after Weston suddenly decided I was surplus to his requirements I had a hunch that maybe he was blowing me off because he was afraid I'd let on about his secret agenda. I always play my hunches, so there you are—that's all I have to say.' He shrugged, thrusting his hands in the pockets of his jacket.

'Thanks for the information,' Rachel roused herself to croak as he turned away.

He gave her a sour grin. 'Yeah, well—consider it my farewell gift. With partners like him, who needs enemies, huh? I'd watch my back, if I were you.'

'Oh, I intend to…'

Rachel watched him walk away into the gathering dusk. She didn't even bother to go into the house. She got back into her car and called Frank on her cellphone, hanging up as soon as he answered. Then she drove over to his place and parked outside, trying to dredge up the courage from her battered soul to take charge of the part of her life that she *did* have the power to control.

As she sat there, staring at the lighted windows in Frank's downstairs flat, the passenger door of the car snicked open and a shadowy figure slid into the seat beside her.

The breath stuttered in Rachel's chest. 'What are you doing here? Did you *follow* me?' She tried to summon some outrage, but all she could achieve was a faint echo of reproach.

Matt's silver-rimmed spectacles glinted in the gloom as he turned his face to hers, his expression sober.

'Lucky for you that I don't take orders well. Were you planning to confront a blackmailer without any back-up?'

She raised her hand to her tight throat. 'You *know*?'

'It's no real big surprise. I've had feelers out with a few contacts—and found out that Frank's the one who's been causing all your petty problems with bureaucracy. It seems that he's been trying to make your private life more stressful on top of loading you up with unnecessary business worries—'

'I went through some back files—found that he'd padded out the quotes on some of the jobs we missed out on in the past couple of years, deliberately pricing us out of contention,' Rachel interrupted numbly. 'But I had no idea that he was behind all that other stuff...' No wonder Frank had been so keen to investigate her mysterious harasser—he never would have tracked down himself!

Matt continued implacably, 'After you left me I called Neville—I threatened to tell Mum and Dad about the real reason Leigh married me if he didn't lay off. He knows that would seriously damage his image with Dad, so he threw me the bone about Frank—said Weston had told him he had compromising photos of you and me but he'd considered it too risky to get involved other than to make an under-the-table agreement that he would hold off granting the security contract he intended to give to WSS until Frank had stirred up sufficient trouble to ease you out of the company. Neville didn't care about Frank's motive—all he was interested in was the by-product: me being humiliated in front of my father, and anyone else he could leak the juicy details to…'

Rachel hunched her shoulders, shivering in the light summer shirt-dress she had donned with such joyous anticipation that morning. 'But…it always seemed so *generous* of Frank to be willing to buy me out if things went wrong…'

'What appears to be generosity is sometimes only ambition disguised. He obviously didn't want to alienate you into a costly open fight over ownership of the business. Instead he kept the value of it carefully depressed. You'd probably have found that after you'd sold out business suddenly picked up again…'

Rachel looked straight ahead, her hands clenched in her lap. She wanted nothing more than to bury her face in Matt's shoulder and bawl out her compound misery. 'I can't put this off. I have to have it out with him.'

'I know. But you're not going in there alone.'

Matt was offering her the kind of bedrock support that she had denied him. She was stricken with shame. 'Thanks, but I don't need you—'

'Oh, yes, you do, Rachel,' he said, with a quiet certainty that skewered her heart. 'You just don't want to admit it yet…'

She turned her head jerkily. He had been brave enough to seek her out after her betrayal of faith; she owed him a similar courage in return. 'I'm sorry,' she choked. 'I shouldn't have reacted the way I did. I know you didn't rape that girl.'

The gravity of his smile was challenging. '*Know?* You've discovered some fresh evidence in the last half-hour?'

Yes, the irrefutable evidence of her love. 'Believe, then...'

She searched for the words to convince him. 'Matt, I don't have to know the details, I—'

He stopped her with a slight gesture of his hand. 'Wait. Let's tackle one problem at a time. First, let's tidy away this business with Frank...'

Her partner took one look at the two of them standing shoulder-to-shoulder on the doorstep and grimaced.

'So you were the hang-up,' he said to Rachel, his blue eyes cynical. 'Checking I was home?'

'Can we come in?' she asked, ignoring his redundant remark. 'We'd like to talk to you about a communication problem you and I seem to be having.'

Frank looked as if he was debating refusing, but he eventually stood back and let them in, following them through to the cramped lounge.

Rachel indicated the computer, scanner and printer in one corner. 'I suppose that would be the gear you used to alter the photos Armstrong gave you. I noticed you purchased some pretty sophisticated image-handling software through the company a few months ago...'

To make sure there was no misunderstanding, she angrily challenged him with the discoveries that she and Matt had made.

To her shock Frank produced no belligerent bluster to dispute the facts. If anything he looked relieved to have it out in the open.

'I guess you're a better detective than either of us ever thought, then, huh?' he said.

'You're not even going to *try* to deny it?' Rachel asked painfully, aware of Matt's solid warmth at her back.

'What's the point? To tell you the truth, I'm sick of the whole mess,' he said, running his hand through his sun-streaked blond hair. 'I never expected to go this far...things just seemed to escalate when you wouldn't bloody well give up the notion of being a full partner...'

Rachel groped for Matt's hand behind her back and held it tightly as Frank continued his self-derisive monologue.

'I was stupid. I don't even know why I did it.' He pulled himself up with a jerk. 'Yes, yes, I do...of course I do.' He mocked himself with an angry laugh. 'It was because I worked damned hard to get where I am today. Dave and I started Westons—the two of us—and we agreed that it would *always* be just the two of us... And then Dave went and got himself killed and pulled the rug out from under me. He knew I'd left him *my* share of Westons in *my* will!'

'You weren't married,' Rachel pointed out.

'Neither was David! He could have waited, couldn't he?' he said, with a logic that didn't bear examination. 'He should at least have *asked* me about it first! So, I thought, OK, a silent partner, I can handle that...but then you started insisting on "helping". So I figured to let the business slide just enough that it wouldn't cost me too much when you decided it was all too hard—but, no, instead you announced that you were going try stepping completely into Dave's shoes. I couldn't stop you while you had the deciding share, but I figured if I kept the pressure on I might eventually be able to persuade you it was a bad idea—especially if you were also having hassles with people like the council and the IRS.

'And then Armstrong lucked out with those snaps. It

seemed like the hand of fate. I wasn't looking to do anything illegal, just create enough embarrassment to give me an excuse to demand you resign. And when Stiller agreed to play along, keeping our future prospects looking rocky, that seemed like the icing on the cake...'

'And you couldn't resist decorating the frosting,' Matt crunched out. 'The nudity wasn't enough; you had to add the whip?'

'Yeah, that was purely stupid. I guess I got carried away with my own cleverness. And sending out that second set of photos was even dumber. I mean, I woke up afterwards and thought, What am I *doing*?' He rubbed a hand across his unshaven face. 'I was jeopardising everything I'd worked for—and for what? So I destroyed the negs and prints and hoped the hell it would all go away if I ignored it.

'I even went to see the psychologist I used to work with when I was in the police. I've spent the past week working out that *I'm* the one who's the problem. Hell...the fact is that Dave is dead and I *do* need another partner to share the load. I've just been resenting it so long I couldn't see the wood for the trees... And the stupidest part of it is— Rachel's proved to have far more guts and go than some of the competitors I let get the jump on us...'

'The question is, what happens now?' said Matt, when Frank's well of remorse had run dry. 'Or rather what does Rachel want to happen?—since I think it's her call.'

She struggled with conflicting feelings. 'Maybe I haven't been at it as long, but I've worked hard for Westons, too— I don't want to throw all that away. But after what you've done, I don't know if I could ever trust working with you again,' she told Frank slowly.

'In that case we either dissolve the partnership or I buy you out, I suppose,' he said tiredly, showing no elation at either prospect. 'I guess if you're going to be a rich man's wife you won't even *have* to work...'

Rachel ignored the dig. 'But that would mean you win,' she instantly objected. 'I don't see why you should get away scot-free.'

'I won't—seeing that we have the KR contract in our pockets, the value of your shares has just shot up.'

'What's the matter with Rachel buying *you* out?' suggested Matt, causing both their jaws to drop. 'I think she's proved capable, don't you? And I'd be happy to help her put up the capital. There's no reason why she couldn't run the business herself...'

'Westons without a Weston?' Frank came back to furious life. 'Look, Rachel, don't rush into anything—think things over for a few days. I'm sure we can work something out... OK, I did some bad things, but nothing I can't make up for, and nothing illegal except maybe when I used Dave's old key to get into your place and pinch those photos back...and maybe that redirection thing with your mail...'

'I don't believe the gall of that man!' stormed Rachel as she and Matt walked out onto the footpath a few minutes later. 'Saying that maybe we should be *thanking* him!'

'He's right, though, isn't he? But for him we wouldn't have gone public with an engagement. And unbeknownst to him, by mailing those photos he *did* bring us together. So I guess we could regard him as our unlikely cupid.'

Cupid. As in the god of love.

Rachel halted under a street-lamp, placing a staying hand on his arm. 'Matt,' she said earnestly, as he turned towards her. 'I—I want you to know I admire you more than any man I've ever known!'

This reckless accolade brought an indulgent smile to his lips. 'That sounds extremely promising. Would you care to take that statement one step further...?'

The overhead light threw his eyes under the shadow of his brow, but she knew they were fixed on her flushed face. She didn't blame him for mocking her. 'I know you probably won't believe I love you—'

'Any more than you dare believe that I love you?'

'After the way I failed my first test of faith.' She faltered under his tenderly caressing tone. 'Everything was so right and then I let it all go wrong.'

'Some very wise and wonderful woman once told me that what goes wrong in one's life doesn't always turn out to be all for the worst.' He reminded her of her own words as he picked up both her hands and carried them separately to his warm lips. 'In fact, sometimes it can force us to be at our best. You were right to be angry with me. I *should* have been as open with you as you were with me. I don't want to have any more secrets from you.'

Her hands tightened on his, her eyes shining with tears. 'I told you, I don't need you to explain.'

'But I need to say the things I should have said before. I need you to know that your faith in me is justified.' His voice became rougher, more choppy, as he told her about the alleged rape that had ended his boyhood and blunted his burgeoning sexual curiosity.

'It was nothing dramatic—just a silly girl lying to cover up the fact she'd been having sex. Her boyfriend got rough one night after a dance, and when her parents caught her sneaking home she panicked and claimed she'd been attacked. When her parents called the police she didn't want to get her boyfriend into trouble so she pointed the finger at me, because I'd been at the dance and she'd seen me leaving on my own about the time she and her boyfriend took off on his motorcycle. She swore black and blue that she'd been a virgin and I'd threatened to kill her if she told anyone what I'd done.'

Now it was Matt clinging to Rachel's strong fingers as he sketched out the rest of the ugly story. 'I didn't have an alibi and I was remanded to prison because there were no beds available in the juvenile facilities.' His eyes briefly reflected a glimpse of the shattered boy he had been. 'I was in there for three days.

'I was pinning my hopes on getting out when the forensic testing came through, but—' here he offered her an ironic smile '—all the charges were dropped when a private detective hired by Dad caught the girl and her the boyfriend together, and she confessed. Thank God Mum and Dad stood by me, but it was rough being treated like a sex-fiend when I was only just getting interested in sex. It certainly curbed any urge to experiment. For a while I was scared that any girl who showed she liked me was going to accuse me of rape. Maybe that's partly why I fell so hard for Leigh…her apparent unattainability made her seem safe…

'I had to wait for you to come along to discover the full potential of love between a man and a woman…'

There, in the warmth of the summer night, Rachel fell in love with him all over again. She drew their joined hands against her breast, letting him feel the beat of her steady heart. 'I can't take away the hurt you've already suffered, but I'm glad to be the woman you waited for. I'm just sorry to have given you such a bad time.'

'But with you, even the bad times are good,' he said, not entirely teasing. 'My life has certainly been a lot more exciting since you entered into it.'

'I don't know if I can supply quite this level of excitement on a permanent basis,' she said shakily, and then realised she was being presumptuous.

'So…where do we go from here?' she asked, freeing her hands and looking from her car to his. But he knew she wasn't talking about mere transport.

'Where do you want us to go?'

'I don't care,' she said recklessly, 'as long as we're together. I'd happily spend the rest of my life proving my love to you.'

'Then you'll probably be needing this,' he said, reaching into the inside pocket of his jacket and producing the brazen engagement ring which she had left behind.

'I didn't throw your roses away, you know,' she blurted. 'The yellow ones you sent after the party. I kept changing the water and they lasted for a week...'

'And you kept that prissy note they came with,' he said huskily. 'That gave me the courage to hope. Courage is like love. It has to have hope for nourishment. I couldn't stop thinking of you after that party. I kept hoping that we would run into one another again soon, wondering if I could invent some excuse for calling you...'

He held out the ring. 'Take it. It's yours.'

'But...I don't want to pretend any more...' she whispered.

'Nor do I.' He slid the ring onto her finger. 'So let's do it all over again, this time for real...'

EPILOGUE

WAKING up next to the man you loved was, Rachel decided, one of life's most joyous delights.

'Good morning, husband,' she murmured to the dark-haired man gazing at her with clearly lecherous intent.

'Happy anniversary, wife,' he purred.

Feeling deliciously wicked, she eased on top of him, enjoying the feel of skin on skin…his naked body adjusting to her flagrantly voluptuous contours.

'Six years and you're still as insatiable as ever,' she accused him laughingly.

'Who's on top of whom?' he pointed out, wrapping his arms around her and luxuriating in her eager kisses.

A blinding flash from the doorway had them both freezing in shock. With a squeak Rachel squirmed off her husband, pulling up the sheets.

'A pitcha, a pitcha—, Kevin taked a pitcha!' the dark-headed four-year-old shrieked excitedly, dancing on chubby legs across the bedroom carpet, the expensive instant camera waving precariously in his stubby fist.

He flung himself against the side of the mattress, giggling as a strong, masculine arm reached down to hook him up onto the bed to join his parents.

He bounced up and down in glee as his mother detached the camera from his dimpled fingers and peeled off the film.

'Oh, God!' Rachel blushed as she watched it develop in full, eye-catching colour. 'My son,' she moaned, 'the budding blackmailer!'

'Let me see.' Matt plucked it from her hands and studied

it in amusement. 'Mmm, this brings back some very interesting memories. I'll have to add it to my private collection,' he leered.

'Matt, you don't still have those wretched photos?' she gasped laughingly.

'Of course. They have great sentimental value to me,' he said with a pious look, and then spoiled it by adding slyly, 'I used to sleep with them under my pillow whenever you were away.'

'Well, you won't need them from now on!'

Rachel and Frank had made their difficult peace, going on to build a new, more equal relationship out of the ruins of the old one. Weston Security Services had gone from strength to strength in the past few years, but since Kevin had been born Rachel had cut back her office hours and done an increasing amount of her work from home. Now WSS had merged with another company and acquired two new partners, and she intended to take a complete break for a while, eager to spend more time with her family.

'Mr Mischief,' she scolded Kevin lovingly, as he crawled between them for a hug and a tickle on his pyjama-clad stomach. 'Stick to your own toys from now on!'

'Tickle Mummy's tummy. Mummy's fat!' Kevin chortled at his rude joke as he clumsily patted her swollen abdomen.

'That's not fat, that's your little baby sister,' Matt corrected him, gentling his hand.

'*Sister?*' Rachel's eyebrows rose. 'Do you know something I don't?'

'Well, you've always given me everything I wanted.' He grinned. 'Why stop now? Besides, isn't that what Dad's ordered this time round? "Got to keep the dynasty balanced!"' He mimicked his father's bark.

'It could be twins,' she teased.

His eyes met hers in blissful unconcern. 'Double the love? I should be so lucky...'

And, much to Rachel's delighted consternation—he was!

HARLEQUIN *Presents*

Set in the steamy Australian outback
a fabulous new triology by
bestselling Presents author

Emma Darcy

Kings of the Outback

**Three masterful brothers
and the women who tame them**

On sale June 2000
THE CATTLE KING'S MISTRESS
Harlequin Presents®, #2110

On sale July 2000
THE PLAYBOY KING'S WIFE
Harlequin Presents®, #2116

On sale August 2000
THE PLEASURE KING'S BRIDE
Harlequin Presents®, #2122

Available wherever Harlequin books are sold.

HARLEQUIN®
Makes any time special ™

Visit us at www.eHarlequin.com

HPKING

Coming in June from

HARLEQUIN®

AMERICAN ❖ ROMANCE®

MAITLAND MATERNITY

When two sets
of twins are born at
Maitland Maternity Hospital on
the same day, unforgettable surprises
are sure to follow. Don't miss the fun, the
romance, the joy…as two special couples find
love just outside the delivery room door.

Watch for:
SURPRISE! SURPRISE!
by Tina Leonard
On sale June 2000.

I DO! I DO!
by Jacqueline Diamond
On sale July 2000.

And there will be many more Maitland Maternity
stories when a special twelve-book continuity series
launches in August 2000.

Don't miss any of these stories by wonderful
authors such as Marie Ferrarella, Jule McBride,
Muriel Jensen and Judy Christenberry.

Available at your favorite retail outlet.

HARLEQUIN®
Makes any time special ™

Visit us at www.eHarlequin.com.